THE PROMISED LAND

MARIANNE DELAFORCE

Published by Marianne Delaforce

National Library of Australia. Cataloging-in-Publication Data

The Promised Land

Book 1 of The Promises Series

Delaforce, Marianne (1964–)

ISBNs: 978-0-6486334-0-2 (ebook)

978-0-6486334-1-9 (paperback)

Cover design by Marianne Delaforce

Cover layout by Ally Mosher

Images from AdobeStock.com

THE PROMISED LAND

Book 1 in The Promises Series

Marianne Delaforce

DEDICATION

For my Nana and Mum
The two strongest,
most beautiful women I know.
You have always had faith in me,
believed in me, have inspired me
to be the best I can be and
encouraged me to follow my dreams.
No matter how wild
and outrageous they are.

PROLOUGE

HAT HEAD 1997
AUSTRALIA

All my life I have felt different. Many times I had looked at the photos of the Italian prisoner of war in my mother's old album. Each time I was constantly drawn to his handsome face and each time something stirred inside me, something I could not explain. I had never met him so why did he seem so familiar to me? I wondered ... was there more to this man than just a Prisoner of War? Could he be my father? It was a question that had remained unexplained until now. I never really felt close to the man who was supposed to be my father. I never loved him like you should love your father. I could never work out why. I thought perhaps it was because I hadn't grown up with him. I had not seen him at all between the ages of four and fourteen. Later I used to go and see him more as a sense of duty than love, I also wanted him to know his grandchildren as they grew up and to share in their lives.

Rose stood alone at the top of the headland gazing out to the rough sea. The wind was howling around her and a soft drizzle had started to fall. Oblivious to this, she was lost in the emotions of the past few months. Finding out the truth about her father, losing her mother and now finding her family in Italy. Her life seemed so far away, and almost unreal.

Her whole life had been a struggle as she had helped raise her half brothers and sisters. She had been married at fifteen because she was pregnant to a man she loved. Then, over the next few years, she'd had another two children. Her husband was not the warm loving man she thought she had married. He turned out to be an abusive alcoholic and for twenty six years he made her life hell, until finally she gathered the strength and courage to leave.

Now the letter had arrived from Italy. From the family. At first they hadn't believed her, but her Italian aunt had known the truth all this time and had confirmed that it was true. Rose had three sisters and a brother living in Verona. Sadly her father had passed away twelve years before. Now the family wanted her to come and meet them. They had said that she was a part of their family and she would be welcomed to her father's birthplace with loving arms.

Now those questions that Rose had been haunted by for the past fifty years were starting to be answered. She had thought back to only a few months ago when her mother, Loretta, had been diagnosed with cancer and was told she had only a few months to live. She thought it was time to tell her daughter the truth. After fifty years of silence, and wanting peace before she died, Loretta had decided to tell Rose what had happened all those years ago.

CHAPTER 1

KEMPSEY

JUNE 1996

Loretta lay sweating and weak in the hospital bed with her daughter Rose by her side. She slowly opened her eyes and whispered, "I have to tell you something, this is very important."

"Please, Mum, don't try to speak. Save your energy" Rose urged.

"No, I have to tell you, please let me finish." She gasped for breath. The cancer had taken most of her strength, but she knew she had to tell Rose the truth and there was not much time left. She had kept the secret way too long.

"I don't know how to tell you this. I have wanted to tell you so many times but I couldn't find the words. You know your father?" Rose nodded, "Well, he wasn't your real father." Rose was silent. She didn't know what to say. Was her mother having delusions from the morphine? Could this be true? She tried to focus on what her mother was saying.

"You know that I had an arranged marriage to your father, but I didn't love him. He was a cruel man. When the war was on, there was an Italian prisoner of war sent to our farm to help us. You've seen his photo in my album." Rose nodded, not sure what to say she urged her mother to continue.

"Your father was away a lot and I became very close to Lorenzo. I taught him to read and write English." She paused, "It's a long story and one that I don't have the time or strength to tell you now," her voice was just a thin thread, her mother's hand touched hers, her fingers long and soft. "It's written in my diaries for you to read. You'll find them in the bottom draw of my dresser. We fell in love and ... well ...!" Loretta stopped and took a deep breath, Rose noticed she looked embarrassed.

"It's okay. Mum, I understand. The Italian is my real father, isn't he?"

Loretta nodded, she had tears running down her face. "I should have told you years ago. I don't know what happened to him, I don't even know if he's still alive. I hope I have not left it too long to tell you. I'm sorry Rose, can you forgive me?"

Rose looked at this amazing woman, she had given her life and she had sacrificed so much for her. How could she feel anything but love for her?

"Mum it's okay. I understand and there's nothing to forgive." Rose took her mother's frail body in her arms and they both wept until Loretta fell asleep exhausted.

Rose sat beside her mother's bed, watching her peaceful sleeping face. She had so many questions still to be answered. She knew she had to find the man who was her father. Did she have sisters and brothers? Why had he not come back for her mother and her? So many things now made sense. Now she finally understood why she had never been very close to her father.

A strong gust of biting cold wind brought Rose back from her thoughts. She turned and started to make her way back down the winding gravel track towards her beachside home. She would read the diaries her mother had left her and find out the truth about her Italian family. Rose strode out with a new purpose. She would save up and make the trip to Italy to meet her family and find out all about this man she had never known. This man who was her father, and who she'd never met.

CHAPTER 2

DORRIGO 1938

Loretta helped her sister put on her wedding dress. Today, once again, she was to be the bridesmaid. Loretta was the eldest daughter of seven children. She had two brothers and four sisters and to her shame was the only one not married. Maria looked at her sister with hope. She felt bad that she, the youngest, was married before her older sister. Maria knew that Loretta was finding it hard today of all days. She had helped all her sisters and brothers prepare for their day yet she still had not found someone to marry.

"Don't worry Loretta, you will find someone too soon. The right one hasn't come along yet," Maria assured her sister.

"I know Maria. A knight in shining armour will come along and take me away on his white horse." Loretta sighed wistfully.

Maria turned to her sister. "You have to stop being so choosy, Loretta. You have had many suitors. Some of them were quite nice. Why can't you settle for one of them?"

"Oh Maria I didn't love any of them and I don't want to just settle. When I marry I want my heart to sing and to feel so much love for the man who I marry that I could not imagine living my life without him in it. Like you and Tony. Speaking of Tony, I'd better get you out there and down the aisle. He is waiting for you." Loretta added the finishing touches to Maria's veil and dress, stepped back and looked at her baby sister. She was an absolute vision. One day this will be me, thought Loretta. But now it was Maria's day and time to call her father in to take his daughter down the aisle.

"Are you ready?" Loretta asked.

Maria looked up. Her face was beaming. "Yes, I think so." Maria threw her arms around her sister. "I love you sis and I know one day that I will be doing this for you. Helping you get ready to walk down the aisle with the man you love."

Loretta pulled away from her sister. She could hear the quiver in her sister's voice and she knew that Maria was a little scared. She was only sixteen and about to be married. Tonight she, would become a woman.

"It will be all okay Maria. Tony knows that this will be your first time and he will be gentle and loving with you. There is nothing to be afraid of." She kissed Maria's cheek and wiped away a tear. "Now let's get Papa and get this wedding underway."

Loretta opened the door to see her father was standing at the end of the hall talking to the minister. "We are ready Papa." Her father turned and came towards them. He was a fine looking Italian man and his chest filled with pride as Maria stepped through the door.

"Oh my little girl, you are so beautiful. Are you ready for your Papa to give you away?"

Maria spoke softly "Yes Papa. I'm a little scared but I'm ready."

"Well, let's get you down the aisle" he turned to Loretta. "You know how this goes Loretta. You've done it often enough so lead the way." Her father shot the remark at Loretta with a look of disappointment in his eyes.

She knew it was a disgrace to her parents that she was twenty-three, the eldest daughter and the only one not married. Loretta lifted her head and walked through the door in front of her father and Maria. She would not let her father see the look of hurt in her eyes or the tear running down her cheek.

The inside of the church had been decorated with flowers from local gardens and their sweet perfume filled the air. Loretta made her way down the aisle towards Tony who stood fidgeting from side to side, he looked as nervous as her sister did. Loretta smiled she knew they were a good match and would make each other very happy. The

ceremony was beautiful and there wasn't a dry eye in the church. Maria and Tony made their way down the aisle as husband and wife to the loud cheering of the congregation. Outside, while the photos where being taken, Loretta noticed a tall, stately gentleman standing to one side staring at her. She had never seen him before and wondered who he was. She did not have time to ponder as she was whisked away for more photos and then off to the reception.

The speeches were made and the meal finished. The tables were cleared for dancing, the band started and people crammed onto the floor laughing and enjoying the music. Loretta was feeling a little light headed as she had drunk quite a few glasses of wine during the speeches. She could see her father talking to the same man she had seen earlier at the church. But who was he?

He seemed quite friendly with her father because they were laughing and shaking hands. Suddenly the stranger turned and walked towards her. He was very handsome, his eyes were dark and he had brown curly hair. He wore small gold rimmed glasses and had an air of sophistication about him as he came towards her. His black suit and tie made him look elegant and dis-tinguished. Over his shoulder she could see her father and mother were watching them smiling. He was now standing before her.

"Loretta" his voice was low and quiet.

Loretta was too stunned to speak so she just nodded.

"Loretta, my name is Daniel Bridges and I am a friend of your fathers. He has told me so much about you. I was so pleased that he invited me to your sister's wedding so I could meet you. Your father thought it would be a good idea for us to get to know each other better." He stood waiting for her to say something.

She knew she must reply but what would she say? "Its nice to meet you Mr Bridges" her voice barely a whisper.

"Please call me Daniel." He reached out and took her hand and kissed it and smiled. He chatted away to her but Loretta was only hearing half of what he was saying. What was her father up to? Why did he want her to get to know this man? Daniel was standing there looking and waiting.

"Loretta, would you like to dance?" He held out his hand for her to take. Did she even have a choice? If she did not accept she would look rude and she felt a stirring inside her that she had not experienced before.

Loretta placed her hand in Daniel's and they made their way to the dance floor. Daniel was a very good dancer, he whirled her around the floor as he continued to tell her about his life. He sounded well educated and his aftershave smelt like pine trees. They chatted and laughed and Loretta decided she liked this man. But, there was something there in his smile that was a little dangerous and a quiver run through her. He told her of his plans for his farm and about his family.

"Loretta, am I boring you?" Daniel asked.

Once again Loretta had only been listening to half of what he had been saying. "No, no not at all. I was listening. I'm just a little light headed from the wine earlier and the dancing."

Daniel looked at her with concern. "Would you like to sit down?" His tone was soft and caring.

"Oh no. I enjoy dancing. I don't get to do it often." Loretta thought, not because I don't want to but because I have no one to dance with. They continued to circle the dance floor in silence, each caught up in their own thoughts. Loretta saw her father approach the band and speak to the band master. What was he up to now? Suddenly the tempo changed to a slow romantic tune. Loretta's father looked at Daniel and smiled, from the corner of her eye Loretta could see Daniel return the smile and nod. What was going on? Daniel pulled Loretta close to him, so close she could feel the warmth of his breath on the back of her neck. He smelt good and it was nice to feel a man's arms around her.

Daniel leaned down and whispered in her ear. "You are very beautiful Loretta, I would like to get to know you better. Can we meet for lunch tomorrow?"

Loretta could see her father watching them. He seemed very pleased with himself. Suddenly the realisation hit, her father was setting her up. He was going to marry her off to Daniel. My god what could she do? She could not disobey her father.

"Are you all right? You're shaking Loretta?"

"Yes, I'm just a little cold that's all." She hoped he would believe her even though it was warm inside the hall. "That and maybe the wine and dancing, I think I need to sit down for a moment."

Daniel led her to a seat and went to fetch her a glass of water. "Here this will help" he handed her the glass and sat beside her his arm across her shoulders.

Loretta took a sip trying to calm her shaking hands. "Thank you" was all she could manage. They sat in silence as Loretta thought about what to do. Well she couldn't disobey her father? Did she even like this man? He was slightly attractive and seemed nice enough.

"Are you feeling better?" Loretta nodded. "You haven't answered my question. Would you like to have lunch tomorrow?" Daniel's dark eyes seemed to be pleading with her. He took her hand so gently in his, she could feel her palms sweating.

"That would be lovely, thank you. I will pack us a picnic lunch and we could go down by the river." Loretta looked him in the eyes and smiled. She could see the relief spread across his face.

"Great, I will pick you up at eleven if that's all right? Now, if you're feeling better would you like to dance some more?" He stood holding out his hand.

"Yes, I'd like that." They danced and talked until the early hours of the morning. When it was time to leave Daniel kissed her cheek and said goodbye. She watched as he drove off into the darkness until she could no longer hear the spluttering of the car engine.

Lost in thought she had not heard her father come up behind her. She jumped when he spoke.

"Daniel is a fine man Loretta. He's well off and not too bad looking either, I know he is a lot older than you but you could do worse you know and at your age you cannot be too picky." By the tone of his voice Loretta knew what her father was really trying to say.

She turned and faced her father, she could feel the heat rising in her face.

"Papa, are you planning to marry me off to the first one who will have me?"

"Don't take that tone with me girl. You will show me the respect that I deserve as your father. You are not getting any younger, you're twenty-three years old and still not married. You bring shame to our family. You would do well to take Daniel seriously, he is looking for a wife who will help him grow his farm and give him children and take care of his family. I think he would be a fine husband for you. Do you understand me Loretta?"

By her father's tone and commanding expression she knew that she had no choice. She would have to learn to like Daniel and marry him whether she liked it or not. Loretta sighed, her shoulders dropped.

"Yes Papa I understand." She turned back to stare out into the night.

Her father nodded and walked away. There was no more to say. He had spoken and she would obey as a good daughter should. Loretta stood on the verandah looking at the stars, lost in thought. How quickly her world had changed. She no longer could wait for her knight in shining armour and true love. She was going to be married off to someone her father had chosen for her.

She would learn to like Daniel because she knew he would soon be her husband. After a short courting period she would spend the rest of her life with him. This is not how she wanted it to be. A tear slowly slid down her cheek as she realised her life was no longer in her hands. Her dreams of finding that perfect love and husband was no longer a reality for her.

CHAPTER 3

Loretta awoke to the sound of kookaburras laughing outside her bedroom window. For a moment she had forgotten the events of the night before as she lay listening to the sounds of the farm coming to life outside, another fresh day had begun. She could hear her parents talking in the kitchen and the realisation of last night's talk with her father made her feel sick. This can't be happening, she whispered to herself. It must be a dream but Loretta knew it was no dream. It was now her reality.

The kookaburras laughed again. Maybe they are laughing at me she thought. There was a sharp hard knock on the door.

"Loretta time to get up" her father yelled "don't forget you have a date today. And you need to make a good impression girl so get moving."

She heard his boots clump down the hall and the screen door slam on his way out. Loretta swung her legs out of the bed and resigned herself to the fact that she must obey her father. What else could she do? Run away? Yes, she could run away, but where would she go? How would she survive with no money and nowhere to live? Maybe she could get a job. But she knew her father would come and find her and drag her back to face the inevitable. She would have to make the best of what was about to happen.

She washed her face and pulled her long curly brown hair up into a ponytail. She put on her white dress with the roses on it. The dress came just below her knees. She tied the red sash around her waist and put on her white shoes with the straps. As she glanced in the mirror she thought to herself well I'm pretty enough. I'm smart too. Had she been too picky all these years? She had had many suitors but no one that made her get butterflies in her stomach. Maybe she had read too many books with happy endings. After all, they were just stories.

Her parents had had an arranged marriage and they seemed happy enough even though her father was dominating and her mother never complained. She would talk to her mother and find out how she too could learn to accept her fate.

Loretta walked into the kitchen. The walls were painted a pale blue with blue and white cupboards. The floor was covered in lino all blue and white squares, lace curtains at the windows and a large wood stove. The smell of freshly baked bread and coffee brewing on the stove filled the room. Her mother was standing at the bench putting things into a picnic basket for Loretta to take on the picnic. She looked up as Loretta entered.

"Oh Loretta. You look lovely. You will certainly make that man's heart flutter today." She smiled but Loretta could see there was pain and doubt in her mind.

"Mum how did you do it? Did you love Dad before you married him?"

"No, Loretta. I did not love him. I only met him a few months before we were married. My father chose him for me. I didn't have a say in it. I was only seventeen when I married your father. I've learnt to love him over the years because he is a good caring man, and he has provided well for the family." She sighed. "You will in time learn to love your husband like I did and you will have your own family to love and care for soon." She took Loretta's hand "It will be ok darling, it really will. The sooner you accept that this is your life now the easier it will be."

They finished packing the hamper together. There were sandwiches of silverside and homemade pickles on the fresh bread from the oven, fresh strawberries from the garden outside, butter cake with lovely pink icing and freshly made lemonade. Loretta picked up the picnic blanket just as the sound of a car came up the driveway. She looked outside to see Daniel pull up in a blue Lanchester saloon car. As he climbed out of the car she saw he had a slight limp that she hadn't noticed last night and he was much older than she first thought. He was dressed in grey trousers and a long sleeve white cotton shirt with the sleeves partially rolled up. He was quite handsome she thought to herself. I guess it could be worse.

Loretta opened the door. "Hello Daniel. It's lovely to see you again. I have our picnic lunch ready and a blanket."

"You look absolutely beautiful Loretta." Daniel picked up the hamper and rug and put them in the back seat of the car. "Lets get going shall we? I'm looking forward to seeing this river of yours. It sounds lovely."

She nodded and smiled as Daniel opened the car door for her. She slid in, admiring the lovely leather seats. Daniel started the engine and started down the driveway.

"Well, which way do we go?"

They drove out onto the main road and turned left towards the green and blue mountains. The road was empty, there were no other cars in sight and no one walking along the road to town. Not many people had cars then, motor vehicles were quite a luxury. He drove past the orchards of fruit trees almost ready for harvesting, past the dairy farms with the cows standing in the fields chewing grass, not even lifting their heads as the car sped past.

They only spoke when Loretta was giving him directions. She felt uncomfortable and awkward, her palms were sweaty and the anxiety curled in her stomach. What do you say to someone who is about to be your husband? They turned off onto a smaller dirt road that led to the river. It weaved through the trees and opened up into a small picnic area. Loretta was relieved to see that they were not the only ones there. There was a family by the water's edge with three young children splashing in the shallows and a young couple sitting under the big old fig tree.

Daniel parked the car over on the far side of the picnic ground away from the others and jumped out to open her door.

"Well my lady. Where would you like to picnic?" He had a twinkle in his eye and a warm smile as he held out his hand to help her out of the car. They chose a shaded grassy spot right by a smaller rapid. It had started to warm up a little and the air was still, except for the sound of the bubbling water of the river.

"Let's take a walk along the river first. There's a lovely little waterfall just up this way."

Loretta led the way along the track. It was a little overgrown and uneven and she wished she had more sensible shoes on instead of her good ones with small heels. She did not want to stumble and look silly in front of him. She had to make sure she made a good impression or her father would be most upset.

The track was thin and the maidenhair ferns and low red tinged ferns grew profusely along the sides. There were bush orchids flowering in pinks, purple and white and massive tree ferns towering above them. They came to a small clearing beside a waterfall. The water steeply flowed a few feet over a lip of rock, before twisting into cascades further down the river. It was not very high or wide but it was indeed splendid. Below a kangaroo was drinking at the other side of the small pool of water. He bounded off when they startled him as they approached. There were butterflies everywhere gliding past this way and that, oblivious to the two people who now stood there.

"Well this is stunning. I must say, I would never have known it was here" Daniel seemed impressed.

"Not many people know about this place. It's where I come when I need solitude and time to think."

He turned to her. "Do you need time to think now Loretta?"

She looked at him and blushed and lowered her eyes. She did not know how to reply to this question. It was all too quick, she needed more time. He stepped closer and placed his hand under her chin and lifted her face so she was looking him in the eyes.

"I know your father has told you that I would like to marry you even though we don't know each other, but we have time to spend together to change that. I will not force you to do anything you don't want. Although I really hope that someday you may even love me or just like me a little at least." He grinned sheepishly. "I will take care of you and I will never hurt you, I promise you that."

He was gazing into her eyes and for a moment she thought she saw that flicker again of something dangerous, but his smile was so charming. She had to try to make this relationship work even though he said he would not force her to do anything she didn't want to, he may not but her father would.

"Let's sit here for a moment and chat by the waterfall. It's so lovely." She said, looking away from his searching eyes.

They sat down on the soft green grass. Daniel did most of the talking. He told her of his dairy farm, she could tell he loved it by the way he spoke of it. The farm was at the bottom of the mountains at Gleniffer in the Promised Land. He told her of his plans to buy more dairy cattle and to plough the fields in the valley to grow crops of corn and potatoes. He had come out from England with his parents when he was five. They'd wanted a warmer climate and they'd been told how wonderful Australia was. His parents were quite well off and had bought the farm when he was only ten and he had spent the rest of his life there except when he was away at boarding school. They had lived many years on the farm, but sadly his parents had both passed away a few years ago. His mother had been quite sad that her only child had still not found a wife and someone to give him a family.

Loretta realised that he was much older than she first thought. In fact he was eighteen years older than her. She wondered why a man of his age had not found someone to marry before this as he seemed nice enough. He was good looking and he was well educated. Maybe this wouldn't be so bad after all.

"I'm sorry Loretta, it seems I've done all the talking."

"That's okay, I've enjoyed listening to you, but I'm a little hungry. How about we go back to our picnic?"

They wandered back along the path to the picnic spot and sat down on the rug. Loretta placed the food out onto the rug and handed him a sandwich. They ate and chatted for hours until the shadows started to get longer.

Daniel stood and held out his hand to help her up. "I'd better get you home." They packed up and drove back to her house. Daniel walked her to the door, he bent down and kissed her on the cheek. She could smell his pine aftershave and his lips were soft and warm.

"Thank you for an enjoyable day. I really enjoyed myself. Would you like to come to my farm tomorrow? We would need to start early. It's about an hour's drive down the mountain. I'll make sure I'll have you home before dark?"

"That would be very nice, thank you. I'd like to see your farm. It sounds wonderful."

"Okay I'll pick you up at 7 o'clock in the morning then." He smiled.

Once again she saw something in his eyes she could not quite understand. Don't overthink this she told herself. It's nothing. Daniel drove out of the driveway and she watched his car until it turned onto the main road. She turned to go inside. Her father was standing behind her.

"I trust you were a proper young lady today?" He put the emphasis on young to make the point that she must realise she should take the first suitor that came along now or she would be an old maid.

"Yes Papa, Daniel is coming over tomorrow to take me to his farm. I'm sure that will please you." Her tone was sharper than she'd intended.

Her fathers eyes clouded. "Watch your tone Loretta. You will do what will bring pride to this family and there will be no long courtship either. I expect you to be married within the next three months."

She lowered her eyes and fought back the tears and the great lump forming in her throat. "Yes Papa." She went straight to her bedroom, shutting the door. She threw herself on the bed and buried her face in the pillow and cried herself to sleep.

CHAPTER 4

When Loretta entered the kitchen the next morning Daniel was already there sitting at the kitchen table with her father having a cup of tea. He rose as she entered and smiled.

"Good morning, once again you are looking as beautiful as ever."

"Good morning Daniel, thank you."

He pulled the chair out for her to sit as her mother poured her a cup of tea and handed her some toast. Loretta remained silent as her father and Daniel discussed farming techniques and the impending war that they hoped they would not have to enter into. Daniel pushed his chair back and stood up.

"Well, we must be off. It's an hour's drive down the mountain to the farm" he turned to her father, "I will have her back before dark." Her father nodded and shot Loretta a look that she knew meant be a polite young lady today.

Daniel opened the car door for her and they headed towards the east, down the mountain range towards Bellingen. The scenery was truly beautiful. Every so often you would get a glimpse through the tall gum trees to the valley below. The road was a little rough and winding, the air was fresh and crisp and she could smell the trees and the damp earth after the morning dew. The forest was full of ferns and different sized grass trees commonly known as "black boys." With their black, thick, rough and corky bark and long, narrow leaves crowded together at the top of the trunks. The sunlight was filtered through the trees to the forest floor. Every so often you could hear the birds calling over the purr of the engine. Daniel pulled the car over onto a small gravelled parking bay half way down, right beside a waterfall that cascaded down the side of the mountain then disappeared under the road and out the other side falling all the way to the valley floor.

"We will have a break here for a moment so the engine can cool down a bit as well as the brakes."

Loretta was in awe of this beautiful waterfall. There was a fine mist which created a haze in the sunlight, its drops winking silver and gold and the faintest rainbow.

"When there are heavy rains over the mountains this road is impassable. The waterfall covers the road and occasionally washes it away. It sometimes takes months for the road crews to repair the road."

He walked over to the side where there were beautiful wild orchids growing. They were a vibrant purple. He picked a stem and brought it back to Loretta.

"For you. It's almost as beautiful as you." Daniel held the flower out to her.

She blushed. She was not used to receiving compliments. "Thank you," she paused, "Daniel, why do you walk with a limp?"

His eyes clouded and his smile disappeared. "I was born with one leg shorter than the other so I have always had a slight limp. I was teased about it most of my years at school but it doesn't stop me from doing anything that everybody else can do." He stared at her now. "Does it bother you?"

"Oh no, not at all. It's hardly noticeable" she felt embarrassed now for pointing it out and she did not know what to say next. She had offended him and his mood had changed.

"Okay we've stopped long enough." His voice was gruff. "Time to get going again, we still have a bit of a drive ahead of us." Daniel turned to get back into the car without offering to open her door.

They drove the rest of the way in silence. Loretta watched the scenery as they meandered down the mountainside and into the valley. They slowed at the small town of Bellingen, drove past the shops and turned to cross the jade green river onto a dirt road.

"Not long now, we are almost there. My farm is in Gleniffer and the area is called The Promised Land. The early pioneers gave it that name because it's so beautiful." His mood had seemed to lighten as they got closer to his farm.

The countryside opened up to lush green farmland, where cows grazed in the paddocks as they passed.

On the dams ducks were swimming amongst the water lilies and water hyacinth which were an array of colours. They drove past the community hall and past The Never Never River. The mountains and escarpment still had a shroud of mist on them and the trees a dominant feature of the landscape where she could see grey gums, blackbutts, tallowwood and white mahogany on the higher slopes. In the gullies, there were mostly smaller trees of flooded gums.

Fifteen minutes later they pulled up to an avenue of trees along a driveway which led to the farmhouse. It was small and quaint and had verandahs around three sides. There was smoke rising from the chimney and fruit trees to one side. Planted along the verandah were rose bushes and a well-established wisteria vine that tangled along the beams and disappeared around the back. It created a screen from the sun when in leaf and a thick mass of glorious mauve blossoms for a short while in spring.

"Well this is my farm," said Daniel with pride. He drove through the gate and as he pulled up beside the steps just as an older woman appeared at the door.

"Hello Daniel, and this must be Loretta?" The woman came down the steps and greeted her with a warm friendly hug. She had tight curly greying hair, she wasn't very tall and she had a bright floral apron on over her dress.

"My name is Agnes. I sometimes help Daniel with the housework and cooking. He's always so busy. I live on the farm next door with my husband George."

Loretta instantly liked this short plump woman. Her perfume had a faint smell of roses and she had such an honest, warm, caring smile.

"Come inside dear. I've got the kettle on for a cup of tea and some freshly made fruit cake, I made it this morning. You must be thirsty after your drive?"

Loretta followed her inside. The front door led directly into the lounge area with high walls and a fireplace. There was a large sofa with a velvet rose pattern, two matching armchairs and polished tallowwood wooden floors with a dark brown rug. The sideboard had a vase with fresh roses and it was covered in photos. The house was tidy and a little bit stuffy, you could tell that it was a man's house, there were no signs of a woman's touch anywhere. There were two doors leading off to one side. She presumed these must be the bedrooms, she blushed thinking that one of these would be where she'd be sleeping with Daniel soon. The kitchen was small and the walls were painted in a soft tan. The cupboards were all white with brown trim. There was a wood stove and a small wooden dining table for four in the centre.

"Do you need to use the bathroom?" Agnes asked.

Loretta nodded gratefully.

"Follow me. It's out the back." The kitchen led out onto a small verandah which overlooked the mountains and the creek below. The area behind the house had been fenced into a neat rectangle with a well tendered vegetable garden in the far corner. Down along a pathway with roses growing either side were two small buildings. One consisted of the shower and laundry and the other the toilet. There was a big copper tub full of water with a fire burning underneath.

"That's the hot water. I usually light it every afternoon so Daniel has hot water for his bath after a long day in the fields. I'll wait for you inside, I'll get the tea brewing."

When Loretta returned inside, Daniel and Agnes had set the table with flowered china cups and saucers, a silver teapot, a sugar bowl, a silver tea strainer, a milk jug that matched the cups and a flowered plate with fruit cake.

"Please sit down. How do you like your tea Loretta?" She gestured for her to take the other chair. Agnes had such a warm, lovely aura about her making Loretta feel a bit more at ease.

"Just with milk. No sugar, thank you."

Agnes poured the tea and placed it on the table in front of her with a slice of fruit cake. "It's my own recipe. I'm known around the district for my fruit cake." Agnes looked so proud, imparting that bit of information.

Loretta was pleased that there would be another woman close by. Someone she could talk to when she came to live here, at least it would not be so lonely. They chatted over their cup of tea about the district and the farms.

Daniel stood up and took her hand. "Come on, I'll show you around the farm. We only have a few hours before we have to drive back up the mountain so I can get you home before dark."

The farm was quite large. They wandered over to the dairy, it was small but functional. Daniel told her he had fifty cows and a bull, but wanted to expand the herd. They crossed over the paddock, under the barbed wire fence and past the cows enjoying the lush green grass. They didn't even stop to lift their heads at the two people walking past them down the well worn track to the creek. The creek flowed over a pebbled riverbed, babbling and bubbling, it sprung over the rocks, washing pebbles about in the small rapids down into a pool, deep enough for swimming it then curved its way down around the bend out of sight. Beams of soft light speared down between the paperbark trees that grew along the banks, bathing the area in gold and giving it an air of mystery and magic.

"We always have fresh water here, this creek runs all year round. It comes down from the mountains we drove across this morning. In summer when it's hot this is the best place to cool off. It's also a haven for all sorts of wildlife. I've seen frogs, parrots, possums, kingfishers, kookaburras, cockatoos, ducks, honey eaters and the odd fox. I come down here to photograph them. It requires a lot of patience and you have to sit still and be very quiet for a long time but it's my passion." She nodded entranced with the beauty of it all.

They walked along the ridge, stopping now and then to look across the land, the grass and trees and the tangles of scrub and large, dead stumps that showed where the earliest timber cutters had been. They followed the rough track until they reached the edge of the bush itself. Most of the land was hilly and covered in scrub. They turned to look back over the expanse of land. It had been partly cleared for grazing cattle and in the valley they could see the creek they had just come from. Further up the hill from the house was the milking shed with a yard to hold the cows when they were brought in twice a day to be milked.

To the west, on the horizon was the Great Dividing Range forming a hazy-blue line of low mountains with a few round 'peaks' here and there. In the opposite direction was the blue line of the Pacific Ocean that was a few miles away. The dead stumps that scattered the land were impressive. They were at least ten feet high and ten feet around the middle with notches cut in them for the feet of the axemen or the two men with a long saw who would have felled the big tree. Daniel told her of how the area used to be busy with the logging trade hence all the old stumps that were left behind. Most of the trees here were eucalypts and if you rubbed the leaves together in your hand they gave off that distinctive bright, head clearing smell. The blackbutts had a silver top with a dark coloured, fine-stranded bark nearer the ground. Tallowwood trees and turpentines had their distinctive smelling leaves and the Ironbark trees had tough, twisted strands of bark, steely-grey to almost black, on a very straight trunk.

They spent the next two hours exploring the farm. Daniel told her of his plans to expand the farm, buy more cattle and plant crops. They had been clearing the bottom paddock ready to plant potatoes and corn. Beside the old wooden barn sat a plough, and in the paddock beside that was a large Clydesdale horse. Macadamia and pecan trees stood tall and proud and a vegetable patch full of all sorts of fresh vegetables at the far side of the house.

By the time they arrived back at the house it was almost one o'clock. They had their lunch, which Agnes had ready for them, on the verandah overlooking the mountain. Its peaks looked like arrow heads. Loretta thought to herself I'm actually enjoying this peaceful land and Daniel's company. The farm was lovely and she knew she could make it more homely inside. Maybe this won't be so bad after all. He seems kind and caring. Maybe I will learn to love him and be happy here. They finished lunch and she helped Agnes clean up and wash the dishes. They said their goodbyes and headed back up the mountain to Dorrigo.

Daniel was a gentleman, or so it seemed. He opened her car door and walked her up the steps onto the verandah where he kissed her cheek.

"Thank you for a wonderful day Loretta, I'm looking forward to spending every day with you. Goodnight."

Loretta smiled politely. "Thank you Daniel. Goodnight and drive safely." She turned and walked inside where she knew her mother would be waiting to hear all about her day.

CHAPTER 5

DORRIGO

JANUARY 1939

The next three months flew by. Days were spent working on the farm with her father and in the kitchen with her mother. Visits from Daniel, dress fittings and the preparations for her wedding kept her busy. She hadn't even been asked if she wanted to marry him. It was an arrangement between her father and Daniel. Her feelings didn't matter.

Now here she stood in the little room that was off the side of the church, dressed in the white wedding gown that her mother had made for her. It had a high bodice with lace around her neck, long sleeves with four buttons at her wrists, a large white sash around her waist and a train that flowed out behind. Her sisters had helped with her curly brown hair and had lifted it up with soft curls falling around her face. Her headpiece was a veil with flowers over the top and was now in place. But there were tears in her hazel eyes, knowing that this was it. There was no turning back.

Maria stood in front of her with her bouquet, she too had tears in her eyes. She knew that this is not what her sister wanted.

"I know it's not how you imagined your wedding day to be Loretta, but I'm sure everything will work out for you. Daniel seems kind and gentle. Surely you will learn to love him?"

Loretta smiled and nodded but Maria could see the look of sadness in her eyes and the resignation that this was her life now, her future had been decided by her father.

"Yes, I'll be fine I'm sure, I'll have a wonderful life and lots of kids to care for." Loretta wondered who she was trying to convince? Her sister or herself. Daniel had been attentive and gentle and he had never tried to force himself on her in the last few months. Only a kiss here and there but tonight she would have to give herself to him as his wife and the thought made her shiver.

Her father appeared in the doorway. He looked so handsome in his black suit which he only wore on special occasions. He smiled but there was a sadness in his eyes that she hadn't seen before.

"You look truly radiant and beautiful my girl. Today you make me very proud. Come on girls. They are waiting for us."

The church organ started playing the bridal march. The bridesmaids grabbed their bouquets and left. Her father took her arm and placed it into the crook of his arm. He bent down and kissed her forehead and whispered, "I love you my darling daughter." Then he guided her out and down the aisle to her awaiting husband to be. She felt apprehension and a nervous excitement about what path her life was about to take.

The ceremony was short and before she knew it she was walking back down the aisle and out of the church as Mrs Daniel Bridges. Her family had lined the church stairs throwing rice over them as they left and headed to the town hall for the reception. It was a small affair with only family and a few close friends. The toasts and speeches had been made, the cake cut and they had had their first dance together as man and wife. Then it was time to leave. It was all a blur, Loretta had drunk a few glasses of wine to settle her nerves for what was to come. She had never been intimate with a man before but she knew what to expect, her mother had made sure of that. Loretta just hoped that Daniel would be gentle with her.

Daniel had delayed their honeymoon as they had too much work to do on the farm. He had promised her that they would go away once things had settled down. Tonight they were staying at the Grand Hotel in Dorrigo before heading back to the farm the next day. With its wide verandahs it stood proudly on a street corner in the centre of town. A grand old building with wide corridors and large ornate rooms. As they entered the room she felt sick at the sight of the large four poster bed and started to shake.

Daniel could see that she was nervous and took her in his arms, held her tightly and kissed her gently on the lips.

"I promise I won't hurt you, it will be okay. Just trust me." He stroked her cheek and ran his hand down her arm.

She shivered at his touch; she felt both excitement and apprehension of what was to come.

"I just need to freshen up a little. I won't be long." Loretta went to the bathroom and took off her wedding dress. She quickly showered and changed into the white satin nightgown her mother had bought for her, she let her long brown curls fall around her shoulders. Looking in the mirror at her reflection, she saw a frightened girl looking back at her, her mind was full of thoughts, well this is it. There is no running away now. She was about to give herself to her husband. When she returned to the bedroom Daniel was already in the bed. The bedside lamp cast a soft light around the room. She could tell he was naked underneath the covers. Her stomach turned but this was her life now, he was her husband. She pulled back the covers only enough to slide into the bed. But not enough to expose his nakedness. She had never seen a naked man before and the thought made her quiver. She lay beside him not sure what to do next.

Daniel turned to her and took her in his arms, kissing and caressing her body softly and slowly. The touch of his hands on her skin sent a burst of heat to her core and a moan escaped her lips. Her body started to respond to his touch. She kissed him back and ran her fingers through his brown curly hair. His kisses became more intense and she could feel his manhood becoming aroused. This sent a tingling through her body, sparks shivered along her nerves and her heart began to pound. Daniel reached over and turned out the light. He knew she was nervous and still a virgin and he wanted to make this as easy as he could for her. With the lights out, the tension slowly released from her body. She let her inhibitions go, and lost herself in the passion. Daniel slid her nightgown over her head and then took her as his wife.

CHAPTER 6

BELLINGEN

MAY 1939

Life on the farm was not so bad, Daniel had been gentle and loving over the past few months. She didn't love him but she did care for him. She hoped this would change with time. Everyday she wrote in her diaries, pouring out her feelings and hopes for the future. She kept these hidden from Daniel, she did not trust him with her innermost thoughts. As loving as he had been, she still had an uneasy feeling that there was something more to her husband but she couldn't quite figure out what.

Her days started early. First she had to cook his breakfast before he headed out to bring the cows into the dairy yard for milking with Mathew and Joseph, the two farm hands. Then she cleaned the house, scrubbed the floors, did the washing and tended the vegetable patch which had climbing beans and peas, lettuce and tomatoes and rhubarb which she stewed to make dessert. She fed the calves before preparing lunch which she took down to the paddocks for the men where they were ploughing the soil for the crops. Then it was back to the house to cook and prepare dinner, fill the copper with water and light the fire to boil the water for them to bathe.

They had chickens for eggs and fresh meat, milk from the cows and fresh vegetables from the garden. Loretta baked fresh bread every day, chopped the wood for the stove and then there was mending and ironing to be done. The days all blended together, it was lonely for her here and she missed her family. Agnes popped in now and then to say hello which helped break the boredom and lift her spirits. Daniel went to town every week to get supplies but he wouldn't let Loretta go with him, she had only been to town three times in the five months that they had been married.

The dizziness and sickness came over her. She'd had this every morning now for the past month. She sat down on the kitchen chair and placed her head in her hands hoping it would pass. Daniel's voice startled her.

"Are you okay?" he knelt beside her and placed his hand on hers.

"I'll be fine in a minute, I have been feeling ill for a month now. I think I'm pregnant."

"You're pregnant! I'm going to be a father. That is fantastic my darling!" He lifted her up and hugged her so tightly she could hardly breathe. "Are you sure?"

"I'm pretty sure, I have missed my last two periods and the sickness is only in the mornings, but I'll know for sure once I see the doctor."

Later that week Doctor Muldoon confirmed she was pregnant and about three months along. The sickness passed over the next two weeks and a small bump started to show. Her mother and father had come down for a visit and to help her prepare the things she would need for the baby. It was sad to see her mother leave, she missed their talks and she rarely got to see her family now. It was so lonely for her on the farm, but soon she would have a baby to care for, she would not be lonely then.

Daniel had gone away again with his friends for a few days, he never told her where he was going or what he was doing. The only time she had asked, he had yelled at her telling her that it was none of her business. She was slowly starting to see another side of her husband, so very different to the man that had courted her. Agnes had come around that morning and asked her to go into town with her for the day and they would have a lovely lunch at the cafe by the river and do some shopping.

"Is everything okay at the farm dear?" The older woman hesitated, as though unsure of the words to use.

"Yes, I get a little tired now, and it is lonely. It will be so nice to have a baby to care for."

Agnes looked concerned but she nodded and changed the subject to scone recipes as they drove the rest of the way to town. They picked up their supplies at Halpini and Wheatley's store, it was the biggest shop in town with two floors of merchandise. Loretta bought some white satin, lace and ribbons to make a christening dress for the baby. She loved walking through the store looking at all the beautiful things they had for sale. They took their time over lunch at the cafe beside the park, overlooking the river. They sat in the shaded outside area enjoying the soft breeze. It was a lovely warm afternoon and children were playing in the playground. Loretta smiled, in a few years she would be able to bring her child or maybe children here to play on the swings, she had so much to look forward to. It was so nice to be amongst people. She took her time over her coffee and sandwich savouring the moment. Loretta enjoyed Agnes's company and her gossip of the people in the area.

"We best be heading back to the farm. George will be wanting his tea soon." They paid the bill and headed for home.

"When will Daniel be back?"

"Tomorrow around lunchtime he said."

"Are you sure you are okay here by yourself?"

"Yes, I'm fine and thank you for today, I had a lovely time. Can we do it again soon? Daniel never takes me to town."

Agnes looked at her surprised. "Oh, of course dear. Maybe again next week. We could buy some wool and knit some booties for the baby" she smiled and waved as she drove off.

The next day Loretta was up early. She wanted to have fresh bread cooked and hot water for Daniel when he returned. She was stoking the fire under the copper when he pulled up outside, she could hear his footsteps on the gravel as he came around the side of the house. She looked up expecting a smile instead his face was twisted in anger.

"Hello Daniel. How was your trip?" He strode towards her. "How dare you go into town without me."

"What? But I was with Agnes" her voice trailed off.

"I don't care. You are not to leave this farm unless I say so or I am with you. Do you understand me?"

She had never seen him so angry before, he was shaking and the coldness in his eyes frightened her.

"But Daniel, I was with Agnes and I'm not a child, you can't stop me" she said defiantly. She didn't even see it coming. He slapped her so hard across her face that it knocked her backwards, she tripped over the water bucket and fell to the ground landing on her stomach on the pile of firewood.

"Do not back chat me girl. You are my possession and you will do as you are told. You will respect your husband." Daniel spat the words at her as he stood over her menacingly.

There was a sharp stabbing pain in her stomach. It ripped through her like a hot knife blade. She clutched her belly and screamed. "Oh no, the baby, you've hurt my baby."

Daniel yelled to Joseph to fetch the Doctor as he picked Loretta up and carried her inside placing her gently on the bed. "I'm sorry Loretta. I'm so sorry. I didn't mean it, I promise it will never happen again."

Loretta lay sobbing, clutching her belly, she could feel a warmth between her legs, looking down she could see there was blood all over the sheets, she knew that she was losing her baby and it was his fault. By the time Doctor Muldoon arrived she was drifting in and out of consciousness.

The blood had kept flowing, even with towels placed there trying to help to stem the flow. Daniel sat sobbing beside her, he was sent from the room to fetch Agnes to come over to stay. There was nothing Dr Muldoon could do for the baby, Loretta had miscarried. Dr Muldoon gave Loretta a sedative to calm her down, and then found Daniel in the kitchen, with his head in his hands.

He looked up as the Doctor entered. "How's the baby and Loretta? How's my wife?"

"I'm sorry Daniel. She's lost the baby. Loretta is fine and I've given her something to help her sleep but she will need some care over the next few days. What happened? Loretta said she fell?" There was a question to this and Daniel knew that he did not believe it. So she was protecting him by not saying what really had happened.

"Yes, I startled her when I came around the side of the house. She tripped and fell."

"Mmmm, that doesn't explain the mark on her face then."

Daniel could see that he didn't believe him, but it was none of his business, she was his wife and she would learn to do as she was told.

Agnes came panting through the front door, she was out of breath, she had an overnight bag with her. "Is she okay? The poor dear. I'll stay as long as you need me too. I'll make us some tea, should I take her one?" She turned to the doctor.

"No, let her sleep. I've given her a tablet. That should give her some peace at least until tomorrow morning when she wakes and realises that she is no longer pregnant." He picked up his bag and turned to Daniel. "Let's make sure there are no more falls. Okay Daniel?"

CHAPTER 7

VERONA – ITALY

JUNE 1939

Lorenzo and his brothers were farmers just outside of Verona in the north of Italy. This was their family farm. They had worked everyday beside their father not returning home until late in the evening. Lorenzo had been born and raised on this farm and it had been his life for the past twenty-four years. The Italian Alps behind his home separated Italy from the rest of Europe. Today he stood there and looked at these snow-capped mountains, they looked like someone had sprinkled a fine dusting of white flour on top of them and they were shrouded in mist at the base. He wondered how long it would be before he would see them again as he took in the beauty of the Adige river winding its way around the little church, built of brick and stone with its two cylindrical towers.

The smells coming from the kitchen where his mother was cooking his favourite meal made him sad, tomorrow he would be leaving. He had been conscripted into the Army to fight, he did not want to leave, he didn't want to fight but he had no choice. If he refused he would be thrown in prison. He would be trained and then shipped out to wherever they needed him.

"Lorenzo, dinner is ready, come and wash up. Your sisters will be here in a minute."

His mother stood at the kitchen door waving at him to come in. He took his last look at the beautiful mountains and turned to say his goodbyes to his family. One last meal around the big kitchen table, he would savour this night, who knew when or if he would ever return?

The next day his father drove him to the Verona Porta Nuova railway station. The building contained a central dome and two smaller buildings on one side, the station's interior was decorated with mosaics and it was very grand and beautiful. There were already about forty other men of all ages there saying their goodbyes. Wives were crying and holding babies in their arms. Mothers were giving their sons one last hug hoping they would return. His mother had not come to see him off, she was not an affectionate person. She had said goodbye that morning with a hug and a kiss on the cheek. His father now stood shaking his hand.

"Goodbye son. Keep your head down and do what you're told. You make me very proud today, I will see you when you return."

"I will Papa, and make sure you don't work too hard while I'm gone. Make those brothers of mine pull their weight a bit more. I'll be back before you know it." They embraced and Lorenzo joined the rest of the men on the train headed for Rome and the training camp.

Lorenzo had been assigned to the 132nd division. At five o'clock every morning the alarm sounded for them to start their training. It was endless days of marching, gun drills, learning about the tanks and crawling through the bush learning survival tactics. He already knew how to shoot a rifle, his father had taught all his sons at an early age to respect this powerful, deadly weapon. Most of the men here in training were farmers and all had been conscripted to fight a war that they did not want to be part of, but it was either fight or go to prison. So they would fight.

CHAPTER 8

GLENIFFER

SEPTEMBER 1939

Loretta and Daniel sat at the kitchen table listening to the radio and Prime Minister Robert Gordon Menzies speech, his voice was controlled and sombre.

"Fellow Australians, it is my melancholy duty to inform you officially that, in consequence of the persistence of Germany in her invasion of Poland, Great Britain has declared war upon her, and that, as a result, Australia is also at war. No harder task can fall to the lot of a democratic leader than to make such an announce-

ment. Great Britain and France, with the cooperation of the British Dominions, have struggled to avoid this tragedy. They have, as I firmly believe, been patient; they have kept the door of negotiation open; they have given no cause for aggression. But in the result their efforts have failed and we are, therefore, as a great family of nations, involved in a struggle which we must at all costs win, and which we believe in our hearts we will win ...

It is plain – indeed it is brutally plain – that the Hitler ambition has been, not as he once said, to unite the German peoples under one rule, but to bring under that rule as many European countries, even of alien race, as can be subdued by force.

If such a policy were allowed to go unchecked there could be no security in Europe, and there could be no just peace for the world.

A halt has been called. Force has had to be resorted to check the march of force.

Honest dealing, the peaceful adjustment of differences, the rights of independent peoples to live their own lives, the honouring of international obligations and promises – all these things are at stake.

There was never any doubt as to where Great Britain stood in relation to them. There can be no doubt that where Great Britain stands there stand the people of the entire British world. Bitter as we all feel at this wanton crime, this is not a moment for rhetoric; prompt as the action of many thousands must be, it is for the rest a moment for quiet thinking; for that calm fortitude which rests not upon the beating of drums, but upon the unconquerable spirit of man, created by God in His own image. What may be before us we do not know, nor how long the journey. But this we do know, that Truth is our companion on that journey; that Truth is with us in the battle, and that Truth must win.

Before I end, may I say this to you? In the bitter months that are to come, calmness, resoluteness, confidence and hard work will be required as never before. This war will involve not only soldiers and sailors and airmen, but supplies, foodstuffs, money. Our staying power, and particularly the staying power of the mother country, will be best assisted by keeping our production going; by continuing our avocations and our business as fully as we can; by maintaining employment and with it our strength.

I know that, in spite of the emotions we are all feeling, you will show that Australia is ready to see it through. May God in His mercy and compassion grant that the world may soon be delivered from this agony."

Loretta sat silently. She could not believe it. They were at war. "Will you have to join up and fight Daniel?"

"Don't be stupid woman." He looked at her with malice. "I can't go to war, I'm not classed as fit and able, not with this leg of mine. I just hope that the farm hands don't feel a need to be heroes. It's hard enough as it is around here now with only two men to help on the farm now that we are getting bigger."

Ever since she had lost her baby there was a gloom all through the house. Daniel had become withdrawn and had only spoken to her now when he needed something done. She was still not allowed to go anywhere unless he was with her, and no matter what she did it seemed she could not please him. He even blamed her for losing the baby.

"You will have to start helping more around the farm too, instead of hiding away in the house all day.

You can come down and help plough the creek paddock today we need to get the crops planted before the rains come next month. Come on get your boots on, it won't plough itself."

All day they worked in the hot sun. Loretta was pleased she had on her wide brimmed hat as she walked behind the plough and planted seeds into the newly turned soil. It was hot, tedious work and it made her back ache from all the bending. It was almost dark when they finally returned to the house. Joseph was there waiting for them.

"Hi boss. I've just come to let yet know that I've signed up to the Army. I'm going to fight those bloody Germans. I've just come to collect my things, and if I could get my pay then I'm on my way."

Daniel became furious. "What am I supposed to do now? We are already struggling to get the work done and now all I have is Mathew and her." He glared at Loretta as though this was her fault too. He stormed off towards the barn.

Why did he have to be so cruel? She had just spent the whole day bending and planting beside him in the hot sun. Now she had to light the fires for the stove and copper and cook dinner, was there no pleasing this man? He was nothing like the man who had courted her. Daniel's moods would only get worse now.

She would miss Joseph, he was always so happy and nothing seemed to bother him. He'd make her laugh with his stories and antics, he'd been kind to her and helped her with the outside jobs. Joseph was younger than her and she knew his mother must be distraught knowing her only son would be going to war. This meant she would have more work to do now and she was already struggling trying to get everything done that Daniel demanded of her.

"I will miss you. You take care of yourself and make sure you come back to us and your family." She gave him a quick hug.

"I will." He nodded in the direction of the barn. "You be careful too. He has a mean streak. Make sure you don't get on the wrong side of it." He smiled and waved goodbye as he left. Loretta watched him walk back down the driveway, sadness in her heart at her friend leaving to do his duty for his country. She knew Daniel would be even harder to please now and she would have to watch herself, she had already felt his fist on several occasions when she hadn't done as he had asked. She wished she could run away to war.

CHAPTER 9

Lorenzo had been deployed to Africa as part of the Ariete Division that landed there in April 1941. They had been fighting for eight months now while defending the area of Bir El Gubi near Tobruk from the British and Australian troops. There had been fierce fighting all day the day before, they had managed to repel the enemy once again but he did not know for how much longer they could keep going. Lorenzo was sitting in a puddle of water with his rifle resting on his knees. He was tired and hungry, he was dirty and his clothes were muddy, stained and torn, he was unshaven and covered in sand and sweat. Will this war ever end? he thought. They had strengthened the existing fortifications, built machine gun and anti tank gun posts, built barbed wire barriers, dug holes and trenches and now they could defend in any direction. He leant back against the rough dirt wall, angry, tired and helpless. The rain had been torrential. He thought of his mountains, hoping he would soon be able to return to his family. It was so hot and humid here.

The rain had started to ease off now and Lorenzo's mind wandered. His eyes began to droop as he was so tired, everything around him dissolved. He imagined standing at the base of his beautiful mountains that were covered in snow, the breeze rustling the leaves in the trees and he could feel the warmth of the sun on his face. There was a flash of lightning and a shattering noise. He was startled from his thoughts by a boom as the shell left the gun. There was a loud scream as it passed overhead, then an almighty crash as it burst spewing dirt, sand and stone all over them. The earth was quaking under his feet, debris from more explosions landing close by him. The machine guns started firing again as bullets skimmed past his head.

They were all hungry and with the lack of supplies they were getting weaker. How could they keep defending if they were too weak to fight? He had seen so much death in the last few months. The screams and heart rending cries of their comrades dying, laying out on the battlefield where they could not be reached, made him sick to the stomach. The smell of death was all around him. Yesterday he had held his friend Guiseppi as he died in his arms, he'd been shot by a sniper. The bullet had hit a main artery in his leg, they could do nothing to save him. Guiseppi had bled to death. Lorenzo promised him he would let his family know how bravely he'd fought, and post them the letter Guiseppi had written that morning. He would tell them how much he loved them when he returned home. That's if he ever got to return home himself.

He looked out from his trench. The battlefield was littered with dozens of burning tanks from both sides. Their smoke was slowly rising into the air and drifting away on the desert winds. The tanks came at them again. So did the Australian and British troops on foot. They could not repel them any longer. They were surrounded. He could hear the British yelling sharp, angry words. The soldiers stood there, their rifles and bayonets fixed on them. Their lieutenant shouted for them to put their guns down and surrender. Lorenzo placed his gun on the ground and raised his hands. He'd had enough of fighting a war he did not believe in. The Allies raised their rifles and indicated for the men to walk in front of them.

They were taken to Alexandria in Egypt to a Prisoner of War camp. There were over a thousand prisoners being held here. The living conditions were reasonable with food and water. Finally they could have a wash and get rid of the last few months of grime and death. After a week he was transferred to the Suez camp where the Italians were housed in tents. It was crowded but at least they had food, some biscuits, meat and tea. Everyone was tired and hungry and fights broke out as they all pushed to get to the kitchen for their share of food. *I will endure this. I will see my home again*, Lorenzo told himself. *I will stay strong.*

They were then moved again to Mombasa. They spent eleven months in the camp at Bairagat. Just surviving each day had become an ordeal. The morale of the men was low but they had been told that they were being moved again. This time to Australia, he hoped that this would be a better place to be held captive. The word was out that at least in Australia if you were a farmer you may be placed on farms to help. He hoped he would be chosen. He needed fields around him, not the barbed wire of a prison.

Lorenzo spent Christmas on board the ship "Molten" en route to Melbourne, Australia. Even though they were prisoners, there was an air of excitement about the next part of their journey. He did not know much about the country they were bound for, only that it was a long way from Italy. After four weeks at sea they finally arrived in Melbourne port just before New Years Eve 1943.

They were marched off the ship and taken to the train station. Here they were lined up and magenta coloured uniforms were passed to them. They were told that these uniforms had to be worn at all times. It was to show that they were Prisoners of War.

The train sat, steaming gently, it was fully loaded and there was not a lot of room in each cabin. He was squashed into a window seat on a hard wooden bench. The stationmaster blew his whistle and the train slowly pulled away from the station. It rumbled below them on the track that was taking them to who knows where. Lorenzo tried to sleep but the noise and heat from all the men squashed into a small space made it impossible. He looked around the carriage, some men dozed or stared out the window like him. It was hot, so bloody hot. He wished he could open the window, but when he'd done that before, big smuts had blown in from the train's smoke. He stared out the window again at the changing scenery of trees with giant white trunks that seemed to go on forever, trees, trees and more trees. More trees with a scattering of rocks, bushes and a small ferny creek. Trees and long grass. They passed small towns and glimpses of rocky bluffs. It was a rugged beauty. Then suddenly a movement flickered. They must be kangaroos. He had heard about the strange animals here. The land was so big, so flat, so different from his home in Italy. His eyes became heavy. It had been a long journey and finally he drifted off to sleep.

The train clattered, slowed and jerked to a stop beside the station. The sign said Cowra what a strange name he thought. The railway platform was long and narrow with a line of buildings on one side, these were the ticket office, the waiting room and the station master's office. On the other side of the railway line stretched farmland. They were filed out into lines and marched up the street towards the camp. People yelled at them as they went past. Some even threw tomatoes at them. He could not understand what they were yelling but by the tone of their voices and the expressions on their faces it was obvious they were not welcome here.

They marched the two miles to the camp. It was north east of town and obscured from the road by a steep hill with granite outcrops. The camp consisted of four separate compounds with each designed to hold one thousand prisoners. The four compounds were enclosed within a twelve sided perimeter. To gain access they entered through the double gates that were located at each end which were guarded by two guard towers and two sentry boxes. The thoroughfare separated the camps with the entrance to each compound in the centre. A and C compound held the Italians. B Compound held Japanese and D compound held a composite of Japanese officers, Indonesians, Taiwanese and Koreans. Outside the compound was a separate perimeter fence consisting of three barbed wire fences. At night the lights glared around the barbed wire camp perimeter.

Lorenzo was assigned to his cabin along with 47 other men in C compound. He had noticed the playing fields, vegetable gardens and numerous buildings outside as he marched past. Now he would write home, he needed to let his family know he was okay.

24th February 1944

Dear Mother and Father,

I hope all is well back at home. I am a Prisoner of War in Australia now. I am in a town called Cowra. We are being looked after and I am in good spirits. Tomorrow I am leaving to go work on a farm at a place called Bellingen. I have been told that I will be housed and fed and will earn a little money for working. I will be back doing something I love. I don't know if they farm like we do in Italy but I'm sure it can't be too different. I send my love to you and father. Let everyone know I am okay and I look forward to the day I can return home to my family.

Your loving son

Lorenzo xxx

CHAPTER 10

GLENIFFER

FEBRUARY 1944

The last three years had been very tough on the farm with the war creating a shortage of labour and food rationing, many ordinary household goods and clothes had become impossible to get. Petrol was severely rationed so trips to town were less frequent now. Loretta felt rather cut off from civilisation and from her family, she also had to do a lot of the manual work in the fields. She'd fallen pregnant twice in that time and had miscarried both times. Daniel had become violent and more abusive to her, both physically and mentally but she could not leave. It would bring shame to her family. When she had told her father of the abuse he had told her that she must obey her husband and there would be no talk of leaving and definitely no talk of divorce. Loretta kept hoping that it would get better but he seemed to blame her for the loss of the babies and he became more and more distant and left the farm for days on end not telling her where he was going or what he was doing. She didn't care anymore. At least there was peace when he was away. She felt like she was always walking on egg shells around him.

Today someone was arriving to help with the work on the farm, they had been assigned an Italian Prisoner of War. He would be housed in the shed at the back and he would take on some of the back breaking work that she had been doing.

Daniel strode into the kitchen throwing the newspaper on the table. "Where's my breakfast? We have a big day today, that Italian bloke is arriving soon and I want to put him straight to work. I want to show him who's boss around here."

Loretta placed the plate of eggs and tomatoes in front of him with his cup of tea. They were lucky that they had a vegetable patch at the side of the house which produced masses of tomatoes, cucumbers, potatoes, carrots, beans and herbs. As soon as he finished she cleaned the plates while he read the paper. She knew not to interrupt him.

The sound of a truck pulling up outside made him rise from the table and walk to the door. An Army officer stepped out of the driver's seat and from the passenger seat a man in a magenta coloured uniform emerged. He was about five foot four inches and had a dark complexion with short black wavy hair. As he approached Loretta she could not help but notice his beautiful green eyes. He caught her eye, smiled, then lowered his gaze. He is quite handsome, she thought.

"Hello Mr Bridges. I'm Sargent Cutler and this is Lorenzo Cammarota. He has been assigned to your farm for work duty."

"Good morning Sargent. Please come inside. My wife will make us a cup of tea while we do the formalities." He turned to Lorenzo and pointed to a chair. "You can stay here on the verandah. I'll send you out a cup of tea." Daniel strode inside with the Sergeant behind him.

Loretta placed the tea and cake on the table and pulled a chair out to sit down, Daniel glared at her. "This is men's business, there's no need for you to be here. Go give that bloke a cup of tea, and tell him to stay on the verandah. You speak his language, make sure he understands. He's not to come inside."

"Mr Bridges, there are a few rules you need to adhere to while the prisoner is on the farm." Daniel nodded. "Here is a list. Please read over it and make sure that everyone who works or lives here sticks to the rules. If you do not, we will take him away." The Sargent took a sip of his tea.

"Don't you worry. He will do exactly as he is told. I can guarantee that." Daniel smiled. "He will know who is the master here. Now let us see what these instructions are." He read the letter out loud.

"The Italian prisoner of war is a curious mixture, in that he can be made to give of excellent work if certain points are observed:

1.He cannot be driven, but can be lead.

2.Mentality is childlike; it is possible to gain his confidence by fairness and firmness.

3. Great care must be exercised from a disciplinary point of view for he can become sly and objectionable if badly handled ...

It is necessary that he be well and warmly clad, both in summer and winter ...

It appears that the Italian harbours no grudge or has no feeling of hatred for us as a race ...

A P.O.W. if left to his own devices too long without constant supervision will tend to become lazy and loaf on the job, but this is readily cured by stricter supervision ... The average Italian is keen on sport and likes nothing better than to go rabbiting (not with a gun)."

Daniel smirked and looked up at the Sargent and handed him the plate of cakes.

"Please have another slice of cake."

Loretta took the cup of tea and a plate of fruit cake out to the verandah where Lorenzo was sitting on the step. He stood up as she came out. She gestured him to the small table with two chairs then placed the cups, tea, milk, sugar and cake down. She poured him a cup of tea. He took two slices of cake. They had spoken Italian in Loretta's family home as she was growing up, she was a little rusty but she could make do. "Please help yourself."

He looked surprised. "You speak Italian?"

"Si. My family were from Italy. I was born here but I can speak a little."

"Grazie." He devoured the two pieces of cake. Obviously he hadn't been eating too well lately. "May I have some more cake please?"

Loretta nodded, her face still uncertain of what to expect, she poured him another cup of tea.

"My husband wants to make sure that you understand you're not allowed in the house. We have a shed out the back which is where you will be sleeping. I'll serve you your meals on the back verandah." Loretta felt embarrassed to be speaking to another human being like that. It was degrading and demeaning, but Lorenzo needed to understand so that he did not get on the wrong side of Daniel.

"I understand. The interpreters at camp made the rules clear to us before we left. I can understand a little English but not much." He popped a piece of cake into his mouth.

She was about to ask him more about himself, when Daniel came out the door with the Sergeant following him.

"Thank you Sergeant I will make sure those rules are adhered to and if he gives me any trouble he will be sent straight back to you." They shook hands and the Sergeant turned to Lorenzo.

"Make sure you do as you're told mate or you will be going back to the camp."

Lorenzo nodded. Loretta was not sure he understood what was being said to him.

"Right follow me," Daniel gestured. "I'll show you where you will be sleeping and remember you are not to come in the house. Understood?"

Lorenzo looked at Loretta. She spoke to him in Italian and smiled. He nodded and followed Daniel around the side of the house. He turned and grinned at Loretta as he went around the corner. She felt a flutter in her stomach. She must watch herself. She had heard stories about the Italian men.

The next few weeks were spent showing Lorenzo what he had to do each day and how to use the equipment on the farm. Her hands were scarred and callused from working behind the heavy disc plough, this work made her back ache. Even her elbows ached from having to hold the reins. This was now Lorenzo's job. She trudged behind him now, bending up and down in the furrows of turned dirt, planting the corn seeds.

They planted cow pumpkins between the rows of corn for the cows to graze on after the cobs of corn had been harvested and put into the barn. This would provide feed for the cattle during the winter months when the pastures had little growth. The corn stalks would be disked into the ground which was further ploughed and harrowed several times until a fine tilth was obtained. Then the seed mixture was mixed together with fertiliser and sown, finally a light roller would be pulled over the soil to compact it slightly. After that all they could do was to pray for rain. Her back still ached from the bending but it was easier than trying to control the heavy plough.

Snakes were another problem on the farm and for his own safety Lorenzo had to be educated about which ones were venomous. Loretta had seen a few snakes in the daylight and knew they always beat a hasty retreat when they heard her footsteps. The snakes here were mostly black snakes with white or pink bellies, but there were also quite a few of the red-bellied variety which were a good deal more venomous. There were also a few of the really deadly brown snakes that were hard to spot and you had to be extra careful when clearing timber. Lorenzo had seen the more colourful and aggressive tiger snake and also a death adder with its characteristic flat, diamond-shaped head.

Lorenzo picked up the work quickly and they worked hard from dawn till dusk. Daniel would come and go from the fields barking orders. Very rarely now would he help out with the back breaking work. That was left to Lorenzo, Mathew and herself. If they weren't ploughing the fields or planting they were digging and packing potatoes in hessian bags before the sunlight turned them green. It was back breaking work but she didn't mind, it kept her busy. There were fences to mend, cows to milk, the windmill to keep running to pump the water up to the troughs higher in the paddock and buildings to repair.

As they worked side by side Lorenzo told her about his farm back home, and how they did things similar to here in Australia, but he also had other ideas that could be useful. Daniel made sure she was never left alone with him for too long and Lorenzo was not allowed in the house. He had to wait by the back door of the kitchen for his meals and eat by himself in his room.

It was nice to have someone else on the farm besides Daniel and their farm hand Mathew. She enjoyed their chats and hearing about his home and Italy, and he hoped that one day he would get to return to his family. Lorenzo was keen to learn to speak English so he could talk to the others. It was frustrating for him that he could not understand what they were saying and they could not understand him.

Loretta started to teach him how to read and write in English. This would make it so much easier for them all to communicate. He was very intelligent and picked it up quickly. Daniel was not happy that she was spending time with Lorenzo on the verandah each afternoon after a day in the field, but he conceded that it would save him time when giving orders. Rather than her doing it or waving his hands around which just frustrated him. Most days Daniel would sit at the end of the veranda pretending to read just to keep an eye on them.

93

CHAPTER 11

MAY 1944

It was early May when Daniel told Loretta he was going away for a few days and that Mathew would stay at the farm while he was gone and he would be in charge of the Italian.

"Remember to watch yourself with that Italian and make sure he doesn't come into the house." His voice was threatening and she knew by the underlying tone what it would mean for her if she disobeyed.

It's my house too, she thought. Why does he have to be so controlling?

"I'll be back in a few days. Make sure the fences have been finished by the time I get back." He shouted over his shoulder as he grabbed his bag and headed out the door. She heard the car start and the crunch of the tyres on the gravel as he drove off. Finally she could relax for a few days.

She knew it was no good asking where he was going or who he was going with. That would only make him angry. The fence around the yard where the cows were held whilst waiting to be milked was falling down in places. They had to take out some of the old rotted fence posts and replace them with the new ones they had purchased from the sawmill. It was hot, heavy work and as Lorenzo dug new holes for the posts, he took his shirt off. Loretta could not help notice his muscular body with the sweat running down his back, glistening in the sunlight. His upper body, honed by years of hard work, he was very strong. He looked up at her and she blushed, she'd been caught staring at him.

He smiled and continued to dig the post hole. He was glad thoughts couldn't be heard. They had only known each other for a few months but he liked this woman. More than liked her and his heart was never wrong.

It was just past lunchtime when Mathew came to her. "I'm sorry Mrs but I have to go. My eldest son just arrived on his bike with a message. My wife has taken ill and I need to go help with the kids. I probably won't be back today. Will tomorrow be alright?"

"Of course. We will be fine. Go to your wife Mathew. We will keep working on the fence. I'll see you tomorrow." Daniel would not be happy that she had been left alone with Lorenzo on the farm.

"Mathew, it's probably best we don't tell Mr Bridges that I was here alone with Lorenzo. You know what he's like and we would both cop a tongue lashing for it."

Mathew nodded. He also knew that he would probably hit her too. He had seen the bruises she tried to cover up whenever Daniel lost his temper.

"I agree Mrs, I don't want to be on the wrong side of him again, that's for sure." He took a few steps and turned. "I'll make sure I'm back early in the morning."

They worked side by side until dusk. Now with Mathew gone they would have to work harder to make sure the fence was complete before Daniel got home. Loretta had put dinner on earlier in the day. It had slowly been cooking away while they worked. It was Irish stew. Onions, carrots, potato, gravy and mutton chops long simmered until they were tender. Also green peas fresh from the garden. Dessert was home grown stewed peaches and custard with fresh cream from the dairy.

They sat on the verandah enjoying the sunset over the mountains. The air was so still you could hear the water cascading over the rapids in the creek. A breeze ruffled the water, sending silver lines shimmering along the surface. As the dusk crept in there was an explosion of intense activity by the birds. Little finches and wrens came out briefly from cover and willy wagtails hopped noiselessly around on the ground. The cockatoos screeched and magpies squawked. You could hear the birds rustling in the leaves in the nearby pecan tree as they settled in for the night. They both sat in silence mesmerised by the beauty of the day coming to an end.

"My mountains in Italy are much higher and in winter there is snow on them," he paused wistfully. "They are very beautiful."

"You miss your home. Don't you?" She could hear the sadness in his voice.

"Yes I do. This land is strange and different to Italy but it is beautiful in its own way" he smiled and gazed at her, he wasn't sure if he should ask but he had to know. "Why do you stay with your husband? He is so cruel to you." He reached out and touched her hand.

She felt goosebumps and the hair rise on her bare arms.

"You are so beautiful, and if you were my wife I would treat you like a princess."

She felt the warmth of his hand on hers and that flutter in her stomach again. She blushed. She knew that she was starting to have feelings for him and it frightened her. She must remember she was a married woman. She pulled her hand away quickly and her blush deepened. She shook her head unsure of how to respond. No one had ever spoken to her like that before.

"He is my husband and I have to do as I am told. It was not my choice, my father arranged the marriage. When I told my father how cruel Daniel was, he said he is your husband and you will do what he asks of you. That was the end of that. My father will not help me." She looked down at her hands in her lap, her shoulders heavy with resignation.

"No man should raise a hand to his wife or any woman. Women are the most precious thing in the world. They bring new life into the world. If he hurts you again I will put him in his place."

"Oh no Lorenzo, you cannot. They will take you away. Maybe even throw you in prison!" She tried to sound firm.

He smiled. "Would you miss me then?" His eyebrows were raised and a cheeky smile spread across his face.

Oh dear, he was so handsome and those green eyes. She blushed. "I have come to care for you Lorenzo. You are always kind and helpful."

He reached for her hand and held it in his. She felt a prickle all over her body. Why did he have this effect on her? She knew she cared for him. Was she falling in love with this handsome Italian? She must watch herself around him, this was dangerous territory.

"We could run away together, I will look after you. I am falling in love with you. We could have a wonderful life together. I would never treat you badly." His green eyes were full of love and she knew he meant it. He kissed the back of her hand so gently.

For a moment she let herself think of what life could be like with him.

"No! We cannot" she pulled her hand away and stood up. "This can't happen. I am married and I have to fulfil my vows even if I don't like it." She turned and ran inside. "I'll see you in the morning. We have to start early to get that fence finished before my husband gets home. Goodnight Lorenzo." She closed the door and leant against it. Her heart was pounding in her chest. She locked the door. Not because she didn't trust him, but because she didn't think she could trust herself.

It was still dark outside when Loretta woke early the next morning. She couldn't sleep because the thoughts of Lorenzo had made her restless. She made herself a cup of tea and sat on the veranda to await the sunrise. As the first light spread, the sounds of life began to multiply. The intermittent hoots and sighs and rattles of the night were replaced by a more persistent chatter, leading to a rush of chirping sounds. The drone of cicadas waking with the sun, the first rays of sunlight flooding the valley and the black wall turning into trees. The sharp clear notes of a currawong, as the soloist in an enormous orchestra of birds calling forth the sun. Daylight glowed up from the horizon. The sky turning blue. The laugh of the kookaburra a short time later left no doubt in her mind that a new day had begun.

There was still a chill in the air and Loretta was glad of her thick jacket and trousers as they walked around the dairy cows and herded them towards the bails which was where they wanted to go anyway because they knew they would find feed there. She breathed in the smells of fresh earth near tree stumps they had dug around. She could also smell very fresh, warm cow dung here and there as each cow got up from her overnight rest. The dew-covered grass glistened in the early sunlight.

Mathew arrived just after they had finished the milking and the cows had been returned to the paddocks to graze. They went straight to cutting more rails for the fence. As they worked side by side, Loretta could feel Lorenzo watching her. There was a funny feeling passing between them. A couple of times their hands touched as they put rails in place, it sent shivers up her arm. How am I going to be able to do this? she thought. She had a strong desire to be with him, but she couldn't.

They stopped for morning tea, Loretta had made a sponge cake with strawberry jam and cream. After they finished Lorenzo went to collect more posts for the fence from the barn. Loretta went to the creek to splash some water on her face. She needed a quiet moment to think and find some peace. She sat watching the water bubble over the rapids.

"Mathew has been looking for you."

She jumped. She had been so lost in thought she hadn't even noticed Lorenzo approach. "He told me to tell you he has gone to town to get more nails to finish the fence. He won't be long." He sat down beside her.

"Loretta I am sorry if I offended you last night and made you feel uncomfortable, but I cannot hide my feelings for you, I am in love with you."

"Please. No Lorenzo I can't." This kind of talk made her uneasy. She knew she too had fallen for him but she could not go there. It was dangerous and out of bounds.

He reached out and caressed her cheek pushing a loose curl back behind her ear. She felt like her whole body was on fire. He gazed into her eyes. She could not look away.

She was mesmerised by those beautiful green eyes. He leant towards her not sure if she would pull away. Instead she leant to meet him, he kissed her softly on the lips. She tasted of tea and sponge cake. His arms were around her now, she strained against his body, she could feel the muscles solid beneath his shirt, her body ached for his touch. Lorenzo kissed her on the cheeks, her forehead and nibbled the side of the neck, her skin was soft and silky to his touch. Loretta was getting lost in the moment. She was trembling. She had never felt anything like this before. Her body felt like it was on fire as he lay her down on the soft grass. This must stop before it was too late.

"Please Lorenzo Stop!" Her voice was just a whisper. The kiss had shaken her. He pulled back from her. Still holding her in his arms he looked at her more closely.

"I know this is wrong but I have never felt like this about a woman before and it frightens me too. I will stop for now, I will wait until you are ready for this, when you want it as much as I do." He smiled that cheeky smile which just made her laugh.

"You are so sure of yourself aren't you?"

He shrugged his shoulders and lifted his eyebrow. "Hey, I'm Italian. Everybody knows we are the best lovers in the world!"

Suddenly they were both laughing. The sound of the truck arriving back at the yards made them jump.

"We must get back." She straightened her hair and shirt. "Mathew will wonder where we are." She strode off towards the house.

Lorenzo watched her walk away. She was such a fine figure of a woman wearing trousers and a loose green cotton shirt and old work boots. She worked as hard as any man and never complained. I will take her far away from here when this war is over. We'll go back to Italy. I will make a family with her and make sure she is loved everyday as she should be loved. He promised himself that he would marry this woman. She was all he wanted even if she didn't realise it yet. And if the boss ever lays a hand on her again I will make sure he will regret it.

For the next two days they worked hard getting the yard finished. Loretta tried to keep her distance as she didn't trust herself. She hoped that Mathew hadn't noticed anything. She knew she was walking a thin dangerous line, but she had never felt so alive. The thought of the kiss by the creek gave her tingles. She shivered at the memory, Lorenzo was watching her. He smiled. He knew what she was thinking about. If Daniel found out he would send him away, maybe even worse. She knew the war would end eventually and he would be sent home to Italy. Could she go with him? Could she leave her home and family and start a new life so far away? Would it even be possible?

CHAPTER 12

JUNE 1944

The day was dead still. The trees were hanging silently above the breathless ground.

It was the start of winter but it was still warm and humid. Daniel had been in a good mood the past few days and had even been nice to her for a change. They had spent the last week clearing the far paddock so it could be cultivated to sew a new pasture for the cattle to graze on. They had cleared the shrubs and cut down trees. The stumps were removed by digging underneath them with a narrow post hole shovel so they could place a charge of gelignite with a detonator in it and a length of fuse. Daniel loved to blow stumps. There would be a tremendous, dull thud and the huge tree roots would fly up into the air landing back down with a crash sending debris everywhere.

The clydesdale horse would then be used to pull the biggest and heaviest ones away to a pile where they would be burnt. Daniel had decided that they would have a day off and they would go to Urunga for the day with Agnes and George. He was even allowing Lorenzo to go with them. They would go to the river and have a picnic lunch. Loretta had cooked a chicken the day before. She placed it into the hamper along with a salad of fresh lettuce, tomatoes, cucumber and onions soaked in vinegar and sugar all from the vegetable patch outside. The bread had cooled on the wire rack for the past hour. She wrapped it in brown paper and placed it on the top so it wouldn't be crushed. There was date and walnut loaf and fresh peaches for a snack.

"Hurry up, I want to get going. What's taking you so long?" Daniel stood in the doorway looking a forbidding figure with his stern expression.

"I'm ready, here's the hamper for our lunch." She handed him the basket, picked up the blanket for them to sit on and grabbed her bag.

Lorenzo was waiting for them outside by the car. Daniel slid into the driver's seat, Lorenzo opened her door for her, she smiled as she climbed in. He grinned and winked at her then sat in the back behind her. Daniel chatted along the way explaining that when springtime approached that they would spread the superphosphate fertiliser onto the new paddock and with the rain that normally came at that time of year it would soon become a lush green pasture.

Agnes and George were waiting for them by the river bank. They had found a spot under a large shady fig tree to enjoy their picnic. It was a pleasant couple of hours enjoying the food and conversation. The men talked about farming, cattle breeding and politics while the two women discussed cooking, recipes and the new fashions.

After lunch Daniel and George headed to the Ocean View Hotel for a couple of drinks and to talk "man's business" as Daniel had put it. Of course

Lorenzo being a Prisoner of War was not allowed inside the hotel.

"Let's take a walk along the boardwalk and walk off our lunch Loretta. Would Lorenzo like to come with us? I guess we can't leave him here by himself." Agnes smiled at Lorenzo.

Loretta translated for him. He shrugged, smiled and followed the women along the pathway. It was lovely and warm but the breeze had started to pick up as they walked along chatting and enjoying the scenery. The wooden boardwalk crossed the junction of the Kalang and Bellinger Rivers as the water rushed in and out with the tide.

"I need to stop for a while dear and catch my breath. I'll sit here while you and Lorenzo walk the rest of the way." Agnes sat on the wooden bench and waved them on.

They continued to walk, marvelling at the beauty of the small seaside town, the Great Dividing Range with its blue, green mountains in the distance and the ocean beyond the river mouth. They stopped at the end and both stared out to sea, lost in their own thoughts. Lorenzo stood close beside her. His hand grasped hers and squeezed. She bit her lip and turned to him. She knew she was falling in love with him but it could not, should not happen. She was a married woman. Even though she did not love her husband she had made a commitment and she had to remember that.

He gazed back at her and she could feel the unspoken words and feelings in his eyes. She knew he felt the same way she did. He lifted her hand to his lips and kissed it softly. She pulled it away but the place where he had touched her burned. Her breath seemed to leave her and her heart was pounding. She clenched her fists so tightly the knuckles were white. It would take all her strength to resist him. Tears pricked her eyes. He was caring and always treated her with respect, something she hadn't had in a long time. She knew she loved him.

"Lorenzo."

"Before you say anything Loretta, please hear me out. You have to know I am in love with you. I know it's only been a short time that we have known each other but I have never met a woman like you before. You are a strong woman even if you don't believe it yourself. You work harder than most men and I know you will make a wonderful mother one day."

She tried to speak. Her face flushed embarrassed by his words.

"I cannot offer you much now except my love and once this war is over I want you to come with me to Italy and start a new life. One where you will be cherished everyday. I will take care of you."

The sound of footsteps approaching bought her back from the spell he was weaving around her. She froze hoping it was not Daniel, she was relieved when Agnes joined them looking out to the sea.

"Oh it's so beautiful. Look at the waves crashing onto the rocks. I can see why so many boats have been sunk here over the years." Agnes seemed oblivious to the electricity passing between them. "Well, we'd best make our way back to the men. They should be ready by now and we still have to go home to do the milking this afternoon." Agnes turned and started to walk back.

"You go Lorenzo. I want to stay a bit longer. I'll catch up. Go please. I need a moment alone to think." He smiled and strolled along beside Agnes back along the way that they had come. Loretta stood facing directly into the now sharp breeze from the sea where the combination of salt spray and tears stung her face. She watched the seagulls' smooth motion as they floated overhead on the breeze gliding effortlessly on the up draughts, it helped soothe her mind.

Could she let this happen? The dream of being truly loved and cared for struck a chord deep in her heart. She hated her life with Daniel. He was mean and uncaring and at times abusive. Maybe, just maybe, it would all work out. Only time would tell. She walked briskly back along the boardwalk to rejoin the others for the trip home.

CHAPTER 13

JULY 1944

Life on the farm had been quite pleasant over the last two months. Loretta and Lorenzo had managed to keep their feelings for each other hidden from everyone. They had stolen a few kisses behind the barn and down by the creek. It felt so good to be with him. Each day Loretta would sit with him for an hour after work and would teach him to read and write English. Daniel complained she was wasting her time on him but he understood it was to make things easier as now

Lorenzo could understand what Daniel was telling him to do.

It was the second week of July when Daniel informed Loretta that he would be going away for a week to look at cattle. He wanted to purchase a new bull for breeding and five more heifers to boost the numbers of the herd. Finally she would have more time alone with Lorenzo. They had been digging and packing potatoes all morning using the large forks. It was strenuous work. A warm breeze was blowing from the south and by lunchtime the wind became stronger and colder. Huge banks of cumulo-nimbus clouds heralded a thunderstorm on its way. Loretta knew it would be raining by nightfall so they would have to hurry to get the potatoes up to the barn.

The storm clouds rolled in over the mountains. The thunder started as a low rumble, then sharp, loud cracks. A white hot jagged bolt of lightning split the chilly sky, and then it was gone. They headed back up to the house, making it to the cover of the verandah just before the skies opened. Mathew was not staying that night. It was his wife's birthday and he had promised he'd be home for her birthday dinner. As

Daniel would not have approved of her being alone on the farm with Lorenzo, Loretta and Mathew had agreed not to tell him.

"I'll be back bright and early in the morning. Lets hope this rain doesn't hang around long." He glanced at the dark clouds. "I'll wait until it clears before I head back over. We can't dig potatoes in this weather."

"Okay Mathew. You drive carefully in this rain and give Mary my love. Please give her this present from me. It's not much but I hope she likes it." Loretta had embroidered a silk handkerchief for Mary with her initials and some small red roses on it. She liked Mathew and his wife. She envied them, they had been married for fifteen years and he was still very much in love with her. "Don't worry I'll be fine and we have work that we can do in the barn if it's still raining in the morning. Now get going before you get into trouble."

Lorenzo was collecting dry firewood from the wood shed, they would need a fire tonight as it was going to be cold. After dinner they were seated in the lounge room in front of the fire. She knew that Daniel would not like the fact that Lorenzo was in the house but he was away and she wasn't going to tell him. They were listening to the news broadcast on the radio about the war in Germany. The fire put a soft glow around the room. She loved the sound of the fire crackling and the smell of wood burning. It felt nice to be so comfortable in her home. Something she didn't have with Daniel.

"Will this war ever end?" Lorenzo sighed. He was beginning to think he would never get to see his farm or his family again. But when it did end that meant he would have to leave Loretta and that thought made him so sad. He must try to convince her to come with him.

Loretta was lost in thought, mesmerised by the crackle and flicker of the fire. She wanted this war to end but that also meant that Lorenzo would be sent back to Italy. She had fallen in love with him. She loved his strength, the way he talked with his hands, the way he stretched out under a tree to rest after lunch, the way he laughed with her and the way he made her feel, kissing her and telling her she was beautiful. She knew it was wrong, but the days were more bearable with him around. They had not taken it any further than the fleeting looks, brief touches and the stolen kisses. It made life easier to bear with him there. She sat quietly on the sofa beside him.

"Loretta, I love you and I do want you to come with me when I return home to Italy. I promise I will take care of you." She smiled and he squeezed her hand. She could hear the truth in his voice.

"I know you would and I love you too, but I am married. I can't see how I could and what about my family? My father would disown me." He stood up and pulled her gently to her feet.

Loretta swallowed hard. A tingle shimmered down her spine. His arms were around her now and she gasped. He pulled her close and she silently cursed the effect his body against her had on her. How could she resist? He kissed her. She tasted passion on his lips and as she wrapped her arms around his neck, he pulled her closer and kissed her more deeply. She melted into his embrace and kissed him back with uncontrolled passion.

"Loretta. Will you lay with me tonight? Come with me to my bed."

She knew it was wrong but she could not escape the feelings of longing for him.

She needed to be with him totally, to give herself to him to be truly loved like she knew she deserved. He grabbed her hand and she followed him to his room. Inside the fire he had lit earlier was burning in the pot belly stove. He struck a match to light the candle on the small table beside the bed. It was just a bit bigger than a single bed but big enough for two.

The thunder rumbled and her blood pounded in her veins nearly as hard as the rain on the tin roof. He turned and looked into her eyes and lent down to kiss her. He found her as hungry for him as he was for her.

His arms were around her waist pulling her closer. Her body seemed to melt against his. He released her hair from the ponytail stroking it as it fell around her shoulders, running his fingers through the soft curls still slightly damp from the rain. "You are so beautiful my darling." He kissed her again. The passion was so intense she could feel her heart beating hard. She responded to his body. His hands travelled up her back and she groaned at the sheer pleasure of his touch. He swept her off her feet, and placed her on the bed.

Parting her hair from her face, he kissed her tenderly on the lips, and slowly started to unbutton her blouse.

Her return kiss was of a passion she'd never felt before. Her body ached. It had been so long since she had been touched. So long since she'd wanted to be. Her entire body tingled to his touch. He kissed her neck and breasts. She shuddered as his hands moved lower down her body removing the rest of her clothes and throwing them on the floor. He stood and undressed. She loved his muscular hairy chest. He lowered himself onto the bed straddling her. She could feel his hardness resting on her inner thigh. A moan escaped her lips. They made love in the light from the fire and it was nothing like she had ever known. She knew that she would love him forever.

Loretta lay in his arms listening to the rain fall on the tin roof and the crackle of the fire. He was asleep beside her. This is how real love was supposed to be, she did not want it to end. She was so confused, she knew it was wrong but how could love be wrong? She was married to another man but she did not love that man, she loved this one. Maybe, just maybe, she could run away to Italy and start a new life. Maybe it was possible. Lorenzo was sleeping soundly. She lightly caressed his face. She loved his dark wavy hair and perfect features. She could hear his soft gentle breathing as she too drifted off to sleep.

It was still raining the next morning when she awoke. She could feel the warmth of his body cuddled into her back, his arm around her holding her close and his breath on the back of her neck. She did not want to move. It felt so good. There would be no potatoes harvested today. Loretta slipped from the bed, dressed and hurried to the kitchen to get the fire burning in the stove so she could cook breakfast and make the tea. Mathew would not be back this morning. Not with the rain. She would have the day with Lorenzo. She could pretend that this was their farm, their home, at least for the day. But there was still work to do.

"It's good to see you smiling Bella." She laughed. It was good to smile. Lorenzo grabbed her playfully and kissed her. Happiness glittering in his eyes.

"Come on" she giggled. "We have work to do here. We will have to clean the barn and fix the shelves. Sit down, I've made you a strong coffee and scrambled eggs. You will need your strength after all that exercise last night."

He winked at her and she couldn't help but smile even wider thinking of how beautiful life could be when you were in love. She smiled a smile of pure joy, entirely her own.

They spent the morning cleaning the barn. In one corner of the barn the smell of harness oil was strong. The leather bridles, collars and harnesses required regular protection with linseed oil and she made sure they were not neglected. Loretta patted the big draft horse's mane. She had come to love this quiet, gentle horse. They needed to move him from the stall so she placed a nose bag holding oaten chaff on him so he could enjoy a quiet munch while they cleaned his stall. They raked the hay, fixed the broken shelves and rearranged the shovels, hoes and rakes into neat piles.

Once again he made love to her in the loft. The rain had eased and the clouds started to disappear. The sun was starting to beat down on the wet land and the smell of wet grass and damp soil made everything fresh again.

Mathew arrived back as she was preparing dinner. "Hi Mrs, everything okay here? No problems?" He looked from her to Lorenzo.

She carefully avoided looking at him in case he could read her thoughts. "No problems Mathew. Everything here is great. We managed to get all the work done in the barn today so if this weather stays good we can hopefully finish the potatoes in the morning before Daniel gets back."

He nodded "I've got my eldest son coming in the morning to give us a hand. It won't hurt for him to miss a day of school. We need the extra pair of hands to get it done before the boss gets back."

"That would be great, thank you. Now, let's have dinner."

Loretta had prepared a roast lamb dinner with roast potatoes, pumpkin, carrots and beans from the vegetable garden. There was fresh fruit salad and jelly for dessert. They sat on the verandah to eat their dinner. The sunset over the mountains was amazing after the storm. Clouds of dusty pink drifting past a slash of molten gold in the sky. They talked about family and farms and what life would be like after this war finally ended.

CHAPTER 14

OCTOBER 1944

Loretta had been feeling sick and dizzy again in the mornings. She knew she was pregnant and she knew it was Lorenzo's baby. By her calculations, it was likely that first night they had made love in his room, the night of the storm. Daniel had not touched her after coming home from his Sydney trip and he had hardly spoken to her for the first three weeks on returning. She was scared, it couldn't possibly be his she thought. She would be due in March. She would have to pretend that the baby was his and early. That's if she could carry full term, she had miscarried four times before. There was a mixture of contradictory feelings swirling in her mind. The anxious uncertainty of the new life growing inside her, the excitement at having Lorenzo's baby, the fear Daniel would work out he was not the father and her strong conviction that this time it would be different. She would do everything in her power to carry this baby full term. Loretta arranged to meet Lorenzo by the creek whilst Daniel was next door at George's farm. She knew he would not be back for at least an hour. Lorenzo was already at their spot when she arrived.

"You are looking radiant today Bella, are you feeling better?"

"Oh yes, I feel wonderful" she kissed him. "I have some news."

She took his hand in hers, then set it over her belly. He looked at her confused. "I'm pregnant," she paused, waiting for the realisation to hit him. "It's your baby, you're going to be a father."

He stared at her. Had he heard her right? A baby, his baby? "Really, a baby? Are you sure?" He looked at her with such love and surprise.

Loretta burst into laughter and his face broke into that broad smile she loved.

"Yes I'm sure it was the very first night that we made love in your room, but we will have to keep it a secret. If Daniel ever finds out who knows what he will do."

The kiss he gave her was the softest, most gentle expression of love she'd ever experienced. He followed by swooping her into his arms, spinning her in a circle and whooping out loud.

"A baby with my beautiful girl, our baby. Now you will come to Italy with me?"

"Yes I will come with you, I don't ever want to be apart from you. We will have our own little family." She was content, finally she would have real love and family. She did not care what her family would think.

"We will have many bambinis Loretta. This will be the first of many" he chuckled and held her tightly. Both were feeling happier than they could ever remember.

Loretta waited another month before telling Daniel. He seemed only mildly interested in the news that she was pregnant again.

"Well, let's see if you can get it right this time. It's not like you can manage to stay pregnant."

He could be so cruel, but his words did not hurt her this time. She didn't care what he said anymore. Nothing could destroy the feeling of pure love she felt for this unborn child. She would carry this baby growing inside her to full term. It had been created with love and this child would be loved.

Agnes was ecstatic, clapping her hands in delight. "Oh Loretta. A baby. I'm sure this time it will be fine. I'll come over more often and help you so that you can rest a bit more." Her eyes crinkled with worry. "Daniel works you so hard and I know he mistreats you. Don't deny it, I have seen your bruises and the marks he leaves on you. You can always talk to me" she said softly. She bent over and gave her a hug.

Loretta knew she could not lie anymore. No one believed her when she kept telling them she was just clumsy and fell over all the time.

"I'll make us a cup of tea and we will make up a roster for what I can do to help you."

Loretta was thankful for her friendship. Agnes had been so good to her over the years. Her only friend really as she was not allowed to go anywhere without Daniel. She was a prisoner here on the farm really. Just like Lorenzo. It would be hard to keep the secret from Daniel but she knew she had to for her sake and the baby growing inside her.

Agnes and Loretta set about making a nursery in the spare room. They painted the walls in a soft lemon colour, made new lace curtains for the window and a floral rug for the floor. Agnes had given her a cane bassinet and a fancy cane pram with a large cane hood that she had used for her children and had no longer any use for. The new cloth nappies had been washed and folded, along with some baby clothes, and placed in the cupboard. Lorenzo had repaired the old rocking chair that they had found in the barn so she could sit and feed the baby. Now it was time to wait for the birth of their child.

She had never felt better. This pregnancy was different to all the other ones where she had miscarried. Her skin was glowing, she slept better, her energy had increased as well as food cravings for unusual things. Whenever they had the chance, Lorenzo would place his hand lovingly on her growing belly and talk softly in Italian to their unborn child. The baby had started kicking and moving and she would laugh at the surprise on his face when it kicked him. Soon, very soon they would have a child to hold and love.

CHAPTER 15

31st MARCH 1945

The first pain came early in the morning. It doubled Loretta up as she stood at the kitchen sink. Her back had been aching all night. She bent, trying to ease the pain. It clutched at her, grabbing her back and hips in one long fierce fire. The baby had not been moving much in the last week and Dr Muldoon had questioned her on her last visit about if her dates for when the baby was conceived were right, as the size of the baby indicated she was further along than what she was saying. The pain hit again and a rush of warm fluid ran down her legs. Her waters had broken. She knew that she would have to get to the hospital. Finally, she had carried a baby full term and she was about to be a mother.

Loretta lay across the back seat of the car as Daniel drove frantically into the hospital. "Slow down Daniel, you're going too fast."

"Well, I don't want you having it in the back seat, I don't know what to do!"

She winced with pain as the car jolted when they hit a pothole in the dirt road. "It will take hours before I deliver but if you keep hitting pot holes at this speed I'm not sure I will last" she cried out in pain. "Please just slow down."

He slowed down enough to ease the jolting of the car and giving more time for him to dodge the holes.

The labour lasted almost all day. Agnes stayed with her, rubbing her back, feeding her ice cubes and encouraging her through the pain. At 4.15pm on the 31st of March 1945 a beautiful, healthy baby girl was placed in her arms. She gazed down at this wonderful new life. A life she had created with Lorenzo. What a miracle! She had a mass of black hair and her face was so pink and perfect. She had a cute little nose and tiny little fingers and toes. She was wrapped in a striped blanket and screaming her lungs out.

Daniel came in looking extremely proud of himself.

"Well finally we have a baby. It's a shame it's not a boy, but at least now we know you can have children so we will keep trying for a boy." How could he say such a thing?

Loretta looked at him. Really looked at him. She realised then how much she disliked this man and thought maybe the reason I haven't been able to carry his babies full term was because of the bad seeds that came from this nasty, hurtful man.

"So what are we going to call her then?"

She gazed down at the tiny bundle in her arms. "I'm going to call her Rose."

"Well, I guess that's as good as anything, I have to get back to the farm, I'll come back when you're ready to come home. I won't be visiting before then as I have too much to do." He turned to leave.

"Do you want to hold her?"

"Oh God no! And can't you shut her up, I hope she won't be screaming like that all the time." He stopped and bent over her looking closer at Rose. "She's big for being a month early don't you think?" he asked.

Loretta lowered her gaze to the baby, now sucking on her little finger. "No, not really. My mother also had big babies. It's the Italian blood." He grunted and left.

The next day Lorenzo came to visit her in the hospital. He'd come into town with Mathew for supplies. He tentatively stuck his head around the door.

"Is it safe to come in? I can't stay long. I told Mathew I had to go to the post office, but I had to see our little girl."

Loretta had just finished feeding the baby so she held Rose out to him. "Can I?" he asked looking a little frightened. "I don't want to drop her." This man who had fought in a horrible war was scared of holding a little baby.

Loretta giggled. "You will be fine. Just hold her head like this." Loretta showed him how to support Rose's head and neck.

He took the tiny bundle in his arms and his eyes filled with tears as he gazed adoringly in wonderment at this child. His child, conceived with love.

"Mia figlia, my beautiful bambina, I promise I will always love you and your mama. I have never felt so much love for anyone in my whole life." He kissed Rose's forehead and handed her back to Loretta. "I must go before Mathew comes looking for me. I will see you when you return to the farm." He squeezed her hand. "I am so proud of you my darling. She is beautiful. Just like her mother. Thank you!" He smiled as he left, before pausing at the door to turn wink and blow her a kiss.

Loretta sat nursing Rose for hours. She could not stop staring at this beautiful baby, touching her little fingers and toes. They were so perfect, she was perfect. It was still sinking in that she finally had a child of her own. She made a promise to herself that she would make sure that her child would have the chance to make her own decisions, choose her own path in life and not be controlled by a man. Rose would be allowed to blossom into whatever she wanted to be.

CHAPTER 16

15th AUGUST 1945

Rose was a good baby. She hardly ever cried, she slept soundly through the night and had done so for the last few months. Her smile lit up the room. She was growing so quickly, where had the last six months gone? Loretta's days now consisted of cooking for the men, cleaning the house and washing, drying and folding clothes. There was so much washing now, the line was always full of nappies. Loretta had never been so happy. A baby to love and stolen moments with Lorenzo whenever they could. He even had the chance to hold Rose when Daniel was not around. His face would light up every time he saw her. Lorenzo had given her a hand knitted silk scarf for Rose. His mother had given it to him before he left for war.

Italy had been fighting with the Allied forces now for almost two years. Just three months ago, the leader of the Nazi Party Hitler committed suicide in his bunker in Berlin on the 30th of April, as the Russian troops advanced towards him and he knew that defeat was imminent. It seemed that soon the war would be over. That meant that soon they would send Lorenzo home. As much as she wanted the war to be over, it would be hard not having him with her everyday and it would take months or even years before she could join him in Italy. It would seem like an eternity.

Rose started to whimper in her bassinet, it was time for her feed. Loretta looked down at this beautiful baby girl. Her eyes had started to change colour. They were going to be green just like her own and Lorenzo's.

"I promise you my darling girl I will never make you marry someone you do not love. You will be free to choose."

She picked her up and held her close. She loved to breathe in that baby smell and would do anything to protect her. At least Daniel had not been abusive to her since Rose's birth. He had not laid a hand on her, but he still yelled at her when the baby cried, telling her to shut that baby up. He wouldn't even say her name. He didn't even want to hold her. It was only when people came over to visit that he made out he was the good father and husband. It was all for show.

Daniel walked in as she was burping Rose over her shoulder and turned on the radio. "What's happening?"

"The war is over, I just had George call in and tell me, it's on the news." The radio crackled and came to life, the voice was Prime Minister Ben Chifley

"Fellow citizens, the war is over.

The Japanese Government has accepted the terms of surrender imposed by the Allied Nations and hostilities will now cease. The reply by the Japanese Government to the note sent by Britain, the United States, the USSR and China, has been received and accepted by the Allied Nations.

At this moment let us offer thanks to God. Let us remember those whose lives were given that we may enjoy this glorious moment and may look forward to a peace which they have won for us."

Loretta's heart sank. This meant that Lorenzo would soon be gone. She was happy for all those families who would soon have their husbands, fathers and sons home from the war but this meant that soon it would be just her and Daniel alone on the farm again.

"I guess this means we will lose our Italian soon then. Which means until we can get some help with the farm you will have to go back to milking the cows again. I'm going to town with a few of the boys to celebrate. Don't wait up. I probably won't be back until tomorrow." He grabbed his things and left. She sat and listened to the car until it turned onto the road and headed into town.

Lorenzo came cautiously in the back door "Has he gone?"

"Yes. He's gone into town. Oh Lorenzo. The war is over. They will take you away soon."

Lorenzo knelt beside her. "Yes, but I will come back for you like we planned, as soon as I can." He took Rose from her and held her in his arms singing an Italian lullaby. Rose looked up at him smiling and reached out her tiny little hand to his face. He rocked her to sleep and placed her in her bed. He reached for Loretta and pulled her into his arms.

"What if Mathew comes in and sees us?" He held her tighter.

"He won't. He's gone home to his family to celebrate. He won't be back until tomorrow." He kissed her with so much passion and love she thought she would burst with happiness. "Soon Bella. Soon we will be together as a family. Very soon."

They sat on the lounge making plans for their future. A future after the war and in Italy on his farm with his family. A life so different to the one she was living in now. A life full of love, hope and happiness.

CHAPTER 17

2nd NOVEMBER 1945

Now as hard as they wished it would not come, the day had arrived. Lorenzo was leaving. They stood holding each other in Lorenzo's room with Rose cradled between them. It was two months since the war had ended and now Lorenzo was being sent back to the Prisoner of War camp in Cowra to await his repatriation back to Italy. Loretta had dreaded this day arriving. The day they would take him away from her. She was not sure she would be able to cope without him there with her everyday. Having him around made her life so much more bearable. Daniel's cruel words now fell on deaf ears because of her love for Lorenzo. She would have to be strong for Rose.

"I'm going to miss you Bella, and this beautiful little angel, but I promise I will come back for you. I will write to you and send you my address when I get to the camp so you can write to me. We will have to be careful what we say in case Daniel gets the letters."

Loretta had tears streaming down her face, her mind unable to accept it. He was leaving tomorrow. She may not see him again for a year or more.

"Promise you won't forget us." She could feel her heart breaking.

"How could I forget you two? You are my world now and we will have a wonderful life in Italy. I promise."

She nodded faintly. There really was no choice at all. She would have to wait. She handed him a photo of her holding six month old Rose in her arms. "Keep this with you and every time you look at it remember how much we love you." He placed it in his wallet, cupped her face in his hands and kissed her. He hoped it would not be too long before he could return and take her away from this place. Back to his beautiful mountains in Verona. He was concerned for her, he'd seen Daniel's temper first hand he was worried that after he left things would get worse for her. He would try his hardest to get back for her as quickly as he could.

The next morning the sky was cloudy and grey and it was raining lightly. It seemed even the sky was crying with her. When the Sergeant arrived to pick him up, Lorenzo was once again dressed in his magenta uniform. He hadn't worn it since the day of his arrival at the farm.

The sergeant exclaimed. "Come on let's get a move on. I have a few more of you blokes to pick up yet."

Lorenzo had said his goodbyes to Daniel and Mathew earlier before they went to do the milking. Loretta handed him Rose for the last time. He gave her a quick hug and kiss on the forehead and handed her back to Loretta brushing her arm with his hand. He wished he could hold Loretta one last time. He knew it would be a long time before he would see her again. He held out his hand shaking hers.

"Thank you Mrs Bridges, it has been my pleasure to work with you."

She could feel his hand trembling in hers. She wanted to go with him now, but she knew that was impossible. She had to be patient.

"It has been a pleasure Lorenzo. Please write to us and let us know how you are and that you have made it home safely."

He winked at her and smiled. "Ciao" he turned and hopped into the car.

Loretta watched the car drive away until she could no longer see them. Her heart sank. Would she see him again? She hoped it would not be too long to wait. She smiled inside as she thought of the flame of love they shared and the happy times spent together and the many more to come when he returned for her.

CHAPTER 18

20th DECEMBER 1945

The food and petrol rationing were expected to continue for some time, but the troops were coming home. The terrible international tension had now been released and it seemed like a much brighter world in which to raise children. A future she hoped would be with Lorenzo in Italy and hopefully for which she wouldn't have to wait too long. She daydreamed of what their life would be like as she stood waiting at the end of the driveway. The old milk can on the gate post was used as the mailbox. She had already checked it but there was nothing in there.

The mail arrived only once a week and Billy the mailman was usually on time but today he must be running late. Loretta was always at the end of the driveway, waiting, hoping there would be a letter from Lorenzo. It had been seven weeks since he had been taken away from her. She could hear the hum and rattle of the mail truck getting closer. Billy pulled up in his old truck. It was an old Ford that had seen better days but it got the job done.

"Hello Loretta, sorry I'm late today, I had a flat tyre." He jumped down from the truck. "Gosh this little girl of yours is growing up fast. She's a cutie just like her Mum." He tickled Rose's chin, she giggled. He handed her two letters. "See you next week, you have a lovely day." He waved as he drove off in a cloud of dust and smoke.

She looked at the letters. One was from her mother and yes the other was from Lorenzo. She recognised his writing. She could hardly contain her excitement, her hands were trembling. She hurried back to the house. She wanted to read it before Daniel came home.

Dear Mrs Bridges

I am still in camp in Cowra and it seems we may be here for a while. There are not enough ships to take us home yet. They have higher priorities than sending us back to our families. We are kept busy here tending the garden or doing repairs on the buildings. I hope you are well and that little Rose is being a good girl for her Mama. I would like to thank you again for your hospitality while I was on your farm. You were very kind to me. Say hello to Mathew and Agnes for me and give my regards to Mr Bridges. Merry Christmas to you and I hope the New Year brings you happiness.
Best Wishes

Lorenzo

P.S It would be very nice if you could write back to me. The address for the camp is on the back of the envelope. Grazie.

Loretta knew that they had to be careful with what they both wrote. He was still a Prisoner of War and their letters would be read by the authorities before they were allowed to be mailed and there was a chance that Daniel may see them. She smiled. She could read between the lines. But the longer it took for him to go home, the longer it would take for him to come back for her. She had to be strong, she had to be patient. But how, she wasn't so sure.

Dear Lorenzo

Thank you for your letter. It was good to hear that you are well. I'm sorry that you are still here in Australia as I am sure you are anxious to be home with your family. Rose is growing so quickly. She is laughing and starting to make sounds. She is trying to talk.

We had a lovely Christmas with a visit from my family. I hope you will be with yours soon. It was our pleasure to have you here on the farm. You were a great help and you will not be forgotten. Mathew and Agnes send their regards. Mathew misses your help on the

farm too as now he is working twice as hard until we can find someone else. I look forward to your next letter when I hope you will be with your family
Kindest Regards
Loretta.

CHAPTER 19

APRIL 1946

When she awoke it was pitch black outside. She and Daniel no longer slept in the same bedroom. Daniel only came to her room now when he had a need or desire an that suited her fine. She hated him touching her, she felt sick every time she heard the bedroom door open as he entered her room. He made her skin crawl. It was like she was being unfaithful to Lorenzo. Outside kookaburras called, then magpies and as the sun rose, the crowing of the roosters began. Rose was still asleep in her cot beside the bed. She lay gazing at this beautiful child, her face so serene and peacefully oblivious to the worries of the world.

She lay there, entranced, feeling tears on her cheeks at the beauty and the wonder that this small child gave her. There were times when Daniel abused her and she felt like she could not go on. It was her love for Rose and Lorenzo that kept her going. Yesterday she had received a letter from Lorenzo telling her about life in camp. He had also sent a belt for her and one for Rose that he had made from cellophane paper. As usual the letters were kept to the same polite conversation between two friends. She wished he could see how much Rose had grown. She would organise to have a photo taken so she could send it to him. Something for him to take back to Italy to show his family his little girl. His own flesh and blood.

No good lying here all day, she thought. She had work to do before Daniel's friends arrived for lunch. Of course he expected her to put on a big spread for his friends and play the happy family. She must get the roast into the oven soon for it to be ready in time. She swung her legs out of bed onto the cold floor quietly, so as not to wake Rose. She made the bed, pulled up the beautiful handmade patchwork quilt her mother had made for her on her last birthday, dressed and made her way to the kitchen to make a pot of tea. Loretta looked out the kitchen window, to where the mountain was glinting in the morning sun. It was another beautiful day, the air smelt of chickens and yesterday evening's rain. She moved the kettle from the side of the stove to the hot plate, it wouldn't take long to boil now. She needed a hot cup of tea before starting her day.

The morning was spent scrubbing and peeling spuds, peeling carrots, chopping pumpkin to peel for roasting and shelling fresh peas. The house smelt of roast mutton, rosemary and pumpkin.

Daniel appeared in the doorway.

"My friends will be here in the next hour. I expect you to have lunch on the table right at midday." He didn't wait for her to reply, he turned and went to the bathroom to clean up.

She had just finished the last of the food preparation when his friends arrived.

Joseph and Fred greeted her as she opened the door with half smiles and a nod. She had met them on several occasions and they rarely spoke to her. She found them to be gloomy and contentious, just like her husband. Daniel came from his room smiling.

"Hello boys. Good to see you. Let's sit down at the table. Loretta, you can serve us lunch now." He spoke to her like she was a servant not his wife.

While they ate, Loretta stayed silent, listening. She knew better than to join in. He only had her there for show. He was Lord of the manor, pretending he had a happy little family. She would have preferred not to be there at all.

She stood to clear the table. "You all go out to the verandah. I'll bring a cup of tea and dessert out to you."

The men rose and made their way outside to the cool afternoon breeze. She collected the plates and placed them on the sink to wash later. Then she placed a generous piece of homemade apple pie in a pool of yellow custard, with fresh cream from the dairy, into four plates. She made a fresh pot of tea and placed cups, the milk jug, sugar bowl and spoons onto the tray. At least while his friends were here he was being civil to her.

When she returned with dessert the talk had turned to the prisoner of war helpers who had been placed on the farms in the area.

Daniel was remarking "The one I had was absolutely useless, and lazy. Not much help at all."

"That's not true Daniel. Lorenzo was a great help around the farm and he was never lazy." She realised as soon as the words came out of her mouth. She should have bit her tongue. Daniel did not like to be shown up in front of his friends. Especially by a woman.

"If I want your opinion I will ask for it. Not that it would mean much." She flicked him a look of disbelief. How could he speak to her like that in front of people? It was a deliberate attempt to humiliate her. Joseph and Fred looked down at the bowls she had placed in front of them.

"This looks great Loretta, thank you." Fred changed the subject tactfully. Daniel shot her a look that she knew. She would have to answer to him later.

Loretta took the plates and cups to the kitchen while Daniel said his goodbyes. She had started to wash the dishes when he came up behind her. His hands closed over her upper arms in a tight grip. She knew she would be bruised tomorrow. His voice was raspy and harsh as he whispered in her ear.

"Don't you ever undermine me in front of my friends again. You're a useless, stupid woman and no one wants to hear what you have to say. Do you understand me?"

She nodded, the menace and viciousness in his voice made her shake inside.

"Next time you do that, I might really hurt you." He stormed out, slamming the door behind him. At least he hadn't hit her this time. Her body and mind felt bruised as if she had been assaulted.

Loretta had never seen Daniel so angry before. She would have to make sure that she never upset him again. She was so tired. She wanted to hurt herself by clawing at her face so the physical pain would stop the pain she felt inside. She couldn't, she owed herself more than that. She would continue on until Lorenzo came back for her and Rose. It was the only thing that kept her going. As she finished cleaning up the kitchen she prayed that it would not be too long before she could leave this place. It may be the promised land by name but it was more like a prison to her.

CHAPTER 20

COWRA

JULY 1946

Lorenzo had been in the camp at Cowra for seven months now. Due to the postwar shipping crisis he was still waiting to be repatriated to Italy. The days dragged on. He wished he could have stayed longer on the farm with Loretta and Rose. Why bring him back to camp if they didn't send him home to Italy? His days consisted of playing cards and tending to the vegetable garden. The formal garden had a water fountain positioned at one end, running into an ob-long pool. There were wooden benches here so they could sit and read or just chat. The fountain had been built by the prisoners who had never left the camp and needed something to fill their days. A reminder of home. On Sundays he went to church and read an Italian novel that had been supplied by the Italian Red Cross.

The camp had facilities with stores, kitchen, mess huts, ablution blocks and latrines, canteens, theatre and recreational huts, barber and tailor shops and medical and dental centres. The large playing field for playing sports always seemed to have someone running around it or teams playing games. Anything to break the boredom of the monotonous day to day life in camp.

Their meals were prepared by Italian Prisoner of War cooks. Hopefully it wouldn't be too much longer before he could get out of here and go back home to tell his family of his plans for the future with Loretta and Rose. He missed them both and hoped that she was not being mistreated by Daniel. It was so frustrating that he could do nothing yet but once he returned home and saved the money he would send for them.

3rd August 1946

Dear Mrs Bridges

Just a short note to let you know I am finally going home. We have received orders that we are to be shipped out tomorrow, bound for Italy. I will soon be back home in Verona once again with my mountains and my family.

I will write to you on my return to my homeland to let you know that I have arrived. Thank you again for being so kind to me.

Kind Regards

Lorenzo

Loretta put the letter down. It had taken two weeks to get to her. He was already on the ship on his way home. It would be months before she heard from him again. The mail from overseas was so slow, sometimes taking four to six months to arrive. It felt like her heart was breaking. Would he keep his promise and come back for them? She could do nothing now but wait.

Agnes knocked before entering. "Hello Loretta, I thought you might like a fruit cake and some company. I know it gets lonely over here for you and I would love a cup of tea and a chat."

Loretta smiled. She loved this stout plump woman with short curly hair, a heart of gold and her big hearty laugh. She was almost family to her. No, she was family.

"Is everything alright dear? You look sad. Has he been hitting you again?"

Loretta looked alarmed. How could she know? She always made sure that her bruises were covered.

"I know dear, I've known for quite some time. I don't understand why some men feel that they need to beat their wives. I'm lucky my George is a sweetheart."

Loretta's eyes filled with tears, Agnes held her while she cried, she couldn't stop crying. "I cannot leave yet," she sobbed. "Daniel would come and find me and drag me back. I'm waiting for" she stopped. She had almost given her secret away.

"Waiting for Lorenzo to come back for you and his child?"

Loretta looked up at her startled. "Yes I know about that too. I will not give your secret away dear. When he was here with you it was the happiest I had seen you in a long time. I could see the way you looked at each other and the way he played with Rose, and there is a resemblance there too. Don't worry. I'm pretty sure no one else has noticed. Men can be so blind sometimes. I will help you get away from here when the time is right. It breaks my heart to see the way he treats you."

Loretta broke into sobs again. She felt a weight lift from her shoulders. She did not have to keep it all bottled up inside anymore. Finally someone to confide in. She knew Agnes would never betray her. She told her how they had fallen in love and yes Rose was his child and he had promised to come back for them both and take them to Italy with him to live. He would write to her when he returned home.

"Okay. When you get his address, write to him and get him to send the letters to me. That way you can be honest with your feelings and make your plans without the worry of Daniel seeing them." Agnes knew they would have to be careful. If Daniel even had the smallest inkling of what was going on. The thought made her shiver. She had seen the bruises and marks on Loretta. She knew what he was capable of.

"Thank you. It has been so good to finally be able to confide in someone. It has been so lonely, and it's hard." She choked on a sob. "Every time I look at Rose I see him looking back at me, I am so grateful everyday for the miracle he has given me in our little girl." They hugged and cried together. She knew she would be able to count on Agnes when the time came to help her escape this life of hell and this loveless marriage.

CHAPTER 21

ROME – ITALY
3rd SEPTEMBER 1946

The ship docked in Rome in the early hours of the morning. As Lorenzo walked down the gangplank, he could smell the fresh coffee brewing and all the familiar smells of his homeland. Finally, after seven years, he was back in Italy. It had changed since he had been away. There were many buildings that had crumbled from where the bombs had landed. He hoped that his home town fared better than Rome. He had not received many letters from his family while he was away and the few he had received only told him of the daily running of the farm and how his family were coping. He did not know what to expect on his return.

Now it was just a train ride back to his beloved Verona. He thought of his first train trip to the camp in Australia and the strange scenery he had seen. This ride would be familiar surroundings to him. He looked around the wharf. There were families everywhere greeting their fathers, sons, brothers and husbands home. Some men were meeting children they had never met, their wives pregnant when they left and were born while they were away at war. His family would be waiting for him back home. He headed for the train station eager to see his beautiful mountains and to tell his family of Loretta and Rose.

The train pulled into the station at Verona, Lorenzo was sad to see that it had been partially destroyed by allied bombings and needed to be reconstructed. He looked out the window and could see his mother and father standing there waiting for his arrival. It had been almost four weeks from the time he had left Sydney, arrived in Rome and taken the train ride to Verona. After all those years away he was finally here. He was happy to be home but there was a deep pang of regret that Loretta and Rose were not with him. He would tell his parents tonight of his love for Loretta and his baby daughter Rose in Australia. He wondered how his mother would take it. She was a very stern, strict Catholic. It was not going to be easy. He'd had time on the ship to think how he would tell them and he had to stand firm. He knew it was not going to be an easy conversation.

His father embraced him and he could see the tears in his eyes. "It's so good to have you home my boy and in one piece. We were all so worried about you."

His mother stepped forward, her arms open and he threw his arms around her as she broke into sobs. She could not speak. Her emotions were too much. He kissed her cheek and nodded.

"I know Mother." Lorenzo threw his back pack over his shoulder and looked at his Father. "Okay, take me home, I need to see my mountains."

Lorenzo stood outside the family home. It was a two story brick building, built in the mid -18th century. The balcony needed some repair. He noticed that they still collected water from the outside fountain as they still had no running water inside. He would have to get onto that. Fix it up to make it better for when Loretta and Rose arrived. The outside fences were falling down and the courtyard had been neglected.

His mother had organised a big family dinner for them that night. It would be good to catch up with everyone and find out what had happened in their lives while he had been away. The table was laden with pasta dishes, risotto, salami, bruschetta, prosciutto, olives, cheese, meat dishes and beer and wine. It was good to be back amongst his family and meeting the nieces and nephews who had been born while he was away. He looked around the table. They were his family, but it was though he didn't know them. They had changed, just as he had in his years away. His father looked old and tired. He would wait until tomorrow to tell them of his plans to return to Australia. Now was not the time.

When Lorenzo walked into the kitchen the next morning his mother was preparing breakfast. His father was seated in his usual chair at the head of the kitchen table.

"Sit down Lorenzo, I have cooked you a big hearty breakfast. You have gotten so skinny you need a good feed."

"Thanks Mama." They sat and chatted about the local news and friends. When they had finished and cleared the plates and were enjoying a freshly brewed cup of coffee.

Lorenzo thought now is the time. He cleared his throat. "Papa, Mama, I have something to tell you. I am in love with a woman in Australia."

His mother's eyes narrowed and her body stiffened. "What? That cannot be!" Her voice was harsh and loud.

"Yes, it is true and we have a child. My daughter. Her name is Rose." His mother's face drained of colour and he could see the anger on her face but she said nothing. "I am going back to Australia to bring them here to live with us."

His father lowered his eyes and fell silent. His mother pushed her chair back and stood up.

"You will not be returning there. Have you forgotten so soon that you were a prisoner there? And you will not be bringing that woman or child to live here in this house."

"But Mama, she is also Italian. She was born in Australia but her parents are originally from Calabria." His voice was pleading now, he needed their blessing.

"I don't care. You will forget her and the child. Do you understand me? You will never speak of her again. I will not have you bring shame on this family by bringing a bastard child here. You will marry a good Catholic girl and stay on this farm and raise your children. That is that and I will hear no more of this nonsense." She stormed from the kitchen to her bedroom slamming the door.

Lorenzo looked at his father "Papa?"

"Sorry son. But you know how your mother is. She will not change her mind."

"But Papa I love her, and she is my child. Your granddaughter. How could she not want her to come and be with family?"

His father stood and put his hand on his shoulder. His smile changed, became deeper, gentler, rich in understanding.

"I'm sorry Lorenzo but I am too old for arguments. I do not have enough strength to fight with your mother. Best you forget this woman and the child and move on with your life. You are home now and I need you to run the farm. I'm not well."

Lorenzo took a good look at his father as he shuffled down the hall to the bedroom. He noticed his father had become much thinner and his skin was sallow. There were dark circles under his eyes.

Lorenzo walked outside down to the river. He looked at his beautiful mountains. I will let it go for now but I am not giving up. He loved Loretta and Rose too much and he had promised her he would be back for them. He could not let them down. He would not break his promise. She was depending on him. He slumped down on the ground with his head in his hands and he wept.

CHAPTER 22

GLENIFFER

DECEMBER 1946

Loretta had taken Rose for a walk to the creek. Along the path there were grass tussocks, bracken ferns and small wattle trees in golden bloom. If you looked closely there were also tiny wildflowers – native violets, forget-me-nots and yellow dandelions. There were larger tree ferns too, some wild raspberry and blackberry vines and the very prickly stems and poisonous leaves of the invasive lantana vine crawling all over other things with its pretty red and yellow flowers. Rose sat dabbling her tiny feet at the water's edge.

Loretta missed Lorenzo so much. At least when he had been here it made it bearable to be around Daniel.

The sound of the creek tumbling between its banks with the murmur of the wind in the gum trees gave her a peace inside. A kingfisher swooped, dived and came up gleaming wet with a small fish in his beak. A duck swam out of the small clump of reeds. She put her hands onto the coolness of the rocks, as if bare skin on rocks might link her even closer to him so far away. They'd had many special moments here on the edge of this creek. Her memories of those beautiful, passionate, loving times and knowing he would come back for them was all that kept her going. She prayed that today there would be a letter from him.

Loretta waited at the gate at the end of the driveway waiting for the mail. It seemed like eternity with mail only arriving once a week. Billy arrived on time today. It had been four months and still no letter from Lorenzo. Hopefully today there would be something.

Billy handed her a letter and a parcel. "Looks like it's from overseas somewhere. It's got funny stamps on it. Maybe it's that fella you had working on the farm here."

She looked at the postmark. Finally word from Lorenzo. "Thanks Billy." She could not wait to get back up to the house to open it. Was he coming back for her? She would soon find out. Once inside she sat at the kitchen table and tore open the letter first.

Dear Mrs Bridges,

I hope this letter finds you , Daniel and Miss Rose well. I am finally back home in Verona. It was so nice to see my family again after so long. Sadly just after arriving home my father passed away. He had been ill for quite some time. My brother told me that he wanted to stay alive long enough to see me home. I have taken over the running of the farm.

My mother is still upset with losing Papa and my brothers have their own family and farms now and cannot help. I wish you could see my farm. Maybe you will one day. Merry Christmas to you all and I hope the New Year brings you all that you desire. Please write back. I enjoy hearing about life on the farm and how little Rose is growing.

Kindest Regards to all
Lorenzo

Loretta opened the package. Inside were two linen towels with beautiful embroidery on them. One with her name and the other with Rose's name. A wall hanging with a picture of the mountains behind Verona. She re-read the letter several times. What did it mean? He had written, *he wished she could see his farm. Maybe one day she would.* Did that mean he had told his family? Was he coming back for her? Or, now that his father had passed away could he not leave the farm. Her heart sank. There was nothing in the letter about how his family reacted to the news of his baby daughter. But she guessed he could not write that in a letter when there was a chance that Daniel may see it. She must write and give him Agnes's address so they could make their plans without Daniel finding out.

Daniel was away a lot lately and he seemed to be angry with her all the time. She could not please him no matter how hard she tried. If he wasn't giving her the silent treatment, he would explode in rage over the most trivial things. It seemed like Daniel received just as much pleasure from hurting her with his words as he did with his fists. Luckily she had not fallen pregnant again. She could not bear the thought of having a baby with him. She only wanted to be with Lorenzo, bear his children and have a family full of love and laughter. She would have to write to him and mail it without Daniel knowing. She needed answers.

Dearest Lorenzo

I was so happy to get your letter and thank you for the beautiful presents. I will treasure them. It seems like an eternity since you held me in your arms, I miss you so much. I am sad to hear of the passing of your father. I am sure it must be a difficult time for you after being away so long from your family.

Daniel is away a lot now which leaves Mathew and I to do most of the farm work. Things are starting to improve here in Australia and are slowly getting back to normal now the war is over.

I miss you terribly. My heart aches for you and your touch. I think of you everyday and the moments we shared together. It is the only thing that keeps me going. Knowing that one day we will be together as a family. Our daughter Rose is growing so fast. She is almost two now and every time I look at her I can see your eyes looking back at me. She loves going down to the creek and paddling in the water and laughing as she chases the butterflies. I am hoping you are still coming back for us. It is the only thing that keeps me going.

How did your family take the news about us? Please write and tell me that you have not forgotten us. I love you with all my heart and cannot wait to see your beautiful Verona.

All our love

Loretta and Rose xxx

P.S. Please write and send the letter to Agnes at her address. She knows about us and will help me to leave when you come for us.

CHAPTER 23

VERONA – ITALY

JANUARY 1947

Lorenzo could not believe how stubborn his mother was being over his desire to return to Australia to bring Loretta and Rose back to Italy. After all, Rose was her granddaughter, his flesh and blood. How could she not want to have her here? He knew she was still hurting after losing her husband three months earlier. Wouldn't she want now to meet her granddaughter even more?

He would continue to work the farm and save enough money, so that even if he could not return, he would send the money to Loretta so she could make the trip to Italy herself. Times had been hard for his family during the war years. There had not been a lot of food available and what they had grown had been taken to feed the troops.

During the war Verona was a refuge for offices of the Fascist regime and as a result was heavily bombed. Verona had been one of the most bombed cities in the area and when the Germans fled in April 1945 they had destroyed the bridges and most of the beautiful old buildings and churches. So many once majestic buildings were now in ruins as well as many houses. Luckily their farm had not been bombed. Some of their Jewish friends had been deported and incarcerated in concentration camps. They never saw them again.

Lorenzo hoped Loretta and Rose were doing okay. It took so long to receive a letter. Anything could have happened to them by the time he received her letters. The thought of Daniel reading his letters made him very wary of what to write. He did not want her getting into trouble because of him. He had to make it cryptic so hopefully she would be able to read between the lines.

Lorenzo spent the day mending the fences down by the river. The horses had knocked them down in a storm one night when the thunder had spooked them. He returned to the house to wash up for afternoon tea. There was a car outside in the driveway which he didn't recognise. He entered through the back door into the kitchen and could hear voices in the lounge room.

"Lorenzo, come in here. There is someone I would like you to meet." What was his mother up to?

In the lounge room sat his mother, another woman about her age, dressed in a black dress and a young woman who looked about twenty five. She wore a pale pink dress and sat shyly on the edge of her chair, her eyes lowered looking at the floor.

"Lorenzo, this is Marguretta and her daughter Paoletta. They live on the other side of Verona. Sit and have coffee with us."

He nodded and smiled at them. "Hello. It's very nice to meet you. Sorry I am a bit dirty from working in the fields today and fixing the fences." He sat in the chair beside his mother as she passed him a cup of coffee.

"That's fine. It's good to see a hard working young man. We don't mind at all. Do we Paoletta?" Marguretta smiled and nudged her daughter. "Say hello dear."

"Hello." She didn't look up at him. She seemed nervous and out of place.

As he drank his coffee he sat quietly, listening to the conversation. "So what brings you here today?" he asked.

"Your mother and I have been talking now for the last few months about your situation." She smiled at him sweetly.

Lorenzo looked confused. What situation? Did they know about Loretta and Rose? Was there something going on his mother had not told him about? He glanced over at his mother then back to Marguretta.

"What situation would that be?"

"Your mother tells me you're single. So is Paoletta. We think that you two would be a good match."

What the hell! His mother was trying to arrange a marriage for him, even though she knew his heart belonged to Loretta and Rose. He glared at his mother. How dare she try to marry him off to the first woman she could find. Would she stop at nothing to keep him from Loretta?

"We are good Catholics and Paoletta is an excellent cook. She can mend and tend house and will make a wonderful mother one day, won't you dear?" She patted her daughter's hand. "She would like to have lots of children." The poor girl was blushing and looked so embarrassed.

"Oh." He struggled to find words. How was he supposed to respond to this without offending her? "Thank you for considering me but at the moment I am really too busy with the farm to consider having a wife right now. Excuse me. There is something I have to do out in the yard before it gets dark. It was lovely to meet you both." He stood and left the room and headed back towards the river. He needed to calm down before confronting his mother.

The sun was setting over the mountains. The pinks, yellow and orange glowed through the clouds and the rays pushed up into the sky. He sat wondering about what Loretta would be doing now. It would be early morning there. A day ahead. She would still be sleeping and hopefully dreaming of him. By the time he had returned to the house it was dark, the car was gone and his mother was standing at the sink washing up the cups.

"How dare you try and marry me off. I'm thirty one years old and I can choose my own wife thank you. You know I love Loretta and my daughter and I will be bringing them here as soon as I raise the money for their fare." His mother turned to face him.

"Don't you speak to your mother in that tone. I gave you life, I looked after you and cared for you and I know what is best for you. You will marry a good Catholic girl, one who has not been touched by another man. "That woman" she waved her hands in the air.

"Loretta, her name is Loretta Mama."

"Whatever. She is not good enough for you. She gave herself to you without being married. That shows she has no morals. She will never be welcome in my house while ever I am alive."

"I love her and she loves me. That's all that matters. I will not let you arrange a marriage for me." He could not contain the anger and frustration in his voice.

"You may be a grown man Lorenzo, but you do not know what is best for you. I do. Don't you ever speak to me again of that woman or that child. I do not want to know them and they will never be welcome here."

He knew he could not argue with her, but he would not let his beloved Loretta and Rose go.

CHAPTER 24

GLENIFFER

SEPTEMBER 1947

There had been no letter from Lorenzo in over nine months. Loretta was starting to despair. She had written to him four times. Maybe the letters were getting lost in the mail. Why had he not written back? Was he alright? What if something had happened to him? Had he forgotten her? Had he found someone else? No, he loved her and their daughter. He had promised he would come back for her. It was that promise that someday he would return for them that kept her going every day.

She was sitting down by the creek with Rose. She spent more and more time there. It was her favourite place on the farm. There were so many beautiful memories of Lorenzo here. Their stolen moments together. She felt closer to him here. Rose had grown so much, so quickly and each day she looked more and more like her father. She was two and a half now. She was chasing the butterflies that were fluttering around in the spring air. Rose giggled as they kept flying away from her every time she got close to them. If only Lorenzo was here to see this. He is missing his daughter growing up. Little things he would not get the chance to see again.

Daniel hardly spoke to her now and when he did it was only to bark orders or criticise whatever she did. She needed to get away, and soon. She did not know how much more she could take. He had flogged her yesterday with his belt because she had stopped him from hitting Rose when she had spilt milk on the floor. Her back was aching from the welts where the belt had landed deep into her skin. She had a gash on her face where the buckle had hit her. She hoped it would heal and not scar. She would make sure no one saw her for a few days until the bruising went away. She could not keep making excuses.

Rose came running over to her "Mumma" she threw her arms around her neck giving her kisses on the cheek.

"Oh Rose. You are a darling, Mumma loves you so much."

"Love Mumma." They giggled and splashed in the water. It was still a bit too cool to swim yet. Soon she would teach Rose to swim when it got warmer. By the time she got back to the house Daniel was there waiting.

"Where have you been?" he bellowed.

"We went down to the creek to chase butterflies."

He stepped towards her and grabbed her arm so hard that she could feel another bruise would soon appear. "You have work to do Loretta. No time to play with the kid. You could at least have given me a son, then he could have taken over the farm." His words cut through the air like boiling water. "You should have been pregnant again by now. Seems you can't do anything properly." He glared at Rose who was clinging to her mother's leg. "She won't be any good for anything. Just like you!" Rose whimpered. "Shut her up for god sake."

Loretta put her arm around Rose protectively and held her tightly. "Shh baby. It will be okay." He had never hit Rose but his temper had been increasing in the last few months. She was not sure of what he was capable of.

"Get in and clean the house up. Then we need firewood cut. I'm going over to the Maxwell's farm to talk to Bob and have a look at the new tractor he just bought. Make sure all the work's done before I get back if you know what's good for you."

She listened to his footsteps leaving, the sound of the car starting and the gravel crunching under the tyres as he drove out the driveway and turned to head north. He would be gone for at least four hours. Hopefully he would have calmed down by the time he arrived back. Rose was still clinging to her leg. She bent down and picked her up and held her tight.

"It will be okay baby. It will be okay. Your daddy will come back for us soon I hope."

As Loretta cut the firewood, a surge of feelings and thoughts flooded her mind. What if Lorenzo had not gotten her letters telling him to send them to Agnes. What if he had written to her here and Daniel had somehow gotten the mail. No, she had always been to the mailbox first. Maybe he had picked the mail up in town before Billy had a chance to deliver it. If he had intercepted a letter he would make sure she knew about it.

"Oh Lorenzo. Where are you? I need you to come and take us away from this." She cried out loudly as she chopped the wood, tears streaming down her face. She promised herself that if Daniel ever laid a hand on Rose she would leave. She would put up with him hurting her, for now but she would not stand for him to hurt Lorenzo's daughter.

If she left, where would she go? How would she support herself and Rose? What choice did she have? She wanted to run away. But if she left, how would Lorenzo know where to find her? No. She would just have to find the strength to continue on until Lorenzo came for her like he promised.

CHAPTER 25

VERONA – ITALY
31st MARCH 1948

Today his little girl would be three years old. It had been over two years since he had seen them. Why had she not written? He had sent several letters but there was still no reply. Maybe Daniel had intercepted them. He hoped he had not. The thought of Daniel taking his anger out on her and his little girl was too much to bear. He looked at the black and white photo of her holding Rose that Loretta had given him when she was six months old. I wonder what she looks like now? She would be walking and talking. I have missed so much. He felt like he had failed them. Just about all the money he made was spent on repairs to the farm. There was not much money left over to save. He had been working endlessly, saving the little money he could but it wasn't enough to pay for their passage to Italy. Then there was his mother. He did not bring up the subject with her again. He would keep writing and saving and then when they arrived his mother would have to accept them. Surely she would not turn them away if they stood in front of her. If she did he would leave the farm and find somewhere else for them to make a home.

His mother had kept trying to push him towards Paoletta. They had visited several times but he always managed to excuse himself with one reason or another. He was in the back shed cleaning the tools. Lost in thoughts of Loretta and Rose.

"Hello Lorenzo."

It was Paoletta. He did not know that his mother had organised for them to arrive today. Maybe because if she had told him she would know he would have made sure he was not around.

"Hello. I didn't know you would be visiting today." He smiled at her. It wasn't her fault their mothers were trying to push them together.

"Neither did I, mother only told me this morning." She paused and looked directly at him. "Lorenzo, don't you like me?"

She stood in the doorway with the sunlight lighting up her hair. She was very pretty, he thought, but she's not Loretta.

"No, I mean yes. You are a lovely woman but." How could he tell her he was in love with someone else? Should he tell her the truth? "Come, let's go for a walk. I need to tell you something." She deserved to know that he could not give her his heart. That she should find someone else. Someone who could truly love her like he loved Loretta.

They walked down to the old tree at the end of the yard and sat on the wooden bench underneath its wide weeping branches. "I'm going to tell you something, and I don't mean to hurt you, but, I'm in love with someone else." He waited for her to respond.

"Oh. Your mother said there was no one else in your life. I didn't know." She looked honestly surprised.

"My mother wishes there was no one else. She will not accept it. I met a woman in Australia when I was there as a Prisoner of War. I worked on her farm. We fell in love and" he paused and took a breath. He didn't want to hurt her. He forced himself to continue. "We have a child together, a girl called Rose and today is her birthday. She is three." He could feel the wetness on his cheek as a tear rolled down. "I miss them so much and I have been trying to save enough money to bring them here to live. My mother has refused to accept them, and has forbidden me from talking about them. That is why she is pushing me at you."

Paoletta was silent for a moment. A surge of feelings and thoughts flooded her mind. "Now I understand why you always disappear when we arrive. I thought you didn't like me. I'm so sorry. Lorenzo it must be hard for you being away from them, and your mother disapproving. Is there any way I can help?"

He could not believe she was so understanding. He had just rejected her, and she now knew his secret and she wanted to help him. He reached for her hand. It was small and soft in his.

"Thank you for understanding. I know it's not fair on you and I should have told you sooner, but no one knows of this, and I wasn't sure how you would react."

She placed her hand on top of his. "Thank you for being honest with me. I am here if you ever want to talk about it. I'm sure it's hard for you with no one to talk to, I promise I will not tell a soul."

He smiled, he felt a weight lift from his shoulders. They chatted for a while longer and then headed back up to the house for afternoon tea. When she left, he kissed her cheek and whispered, "Thank you."

"Your welcome" she smiled and he could see the honesty in her eyes. "Goodbye Mrs Cammarota, thank you for a lovely afternoon tea." He stood watching them drive away.

"About time you came to your senses. She will make you a good wife." He didn't bother to answer her. What was the point? She would only argue with him anyway.

CHAPTER 26

GLENIFFER

NOVEMBER 1948

Agnes held Loretta tightly in her arms and tried to calm her down. She was crying hysterically. "Shh you will wake Rose up. You do not want her to see you upset."

Loretta tried to calm herself. She took deep breaths trying to stop the sobs that kept racking her body. She looked up at Agnes. Her right eye was swollen shut and black. She could hardly see from it, her lip was split and she could taste the blood in her mouth. Daniel had lost control last night and had used her as a punching bag. Her body hurt all over from being thrown around like a rag doll but she had managed to keep Rose out of his way.

"Now tell me what happened." Agnes poured her a cup of Camomile tea and placed it in front of her on the table. "Drink this. It will help. Be careful it is hot."

She sipped her tea. The smell made her feel ill. She tried to keep her voice steady.

"Last night, after dinner, I was cleaning up the dinner plates. Rose was trying to help but she dropped a glass and it shattered on the corner of the fireplace. Daniel was furious. He stood up and hit her across the face and called her a stupid child. She ran screaming to me and hid behind me." She stifled a sob. "He demanded that I give her to him so he could teach her a lesson. She needed to be punished. I said only over my dead body you will hurt her. He smiled that wicked grin of his and shouted "all right then." He punched me in the face and kept hitting me until I fell down. Rose had run away and hidden like I had told her to. Thank god. I thought he was going to kill me." She started to sob again uncontrollably, Agnes held her tighter.

"It's okay. It will be okay. Where is he now?"

"I don't know. He stormed out last night and I haven't seen him since. I have to leave here before he gets back. I will not let him hurt Rose or me ever again. Will you help me?" She looked up at Agnes, her eyes pleading.

"Yes dear. I will pack some things now for you. Do you have any money?"

"A little. I have been saving but Daniel never lets me have any money. He reckons a woman doesn't need it when the man is in charge."

"Ok. We will work something out. Come on. We need to hurry in case he comes back."

They shoved some clothes and personal items into a bag. Loretta made sure she had her diaries, letters and gifts from Lorenzo and his photos. She had not heard from him now for fourteen months but she still prayed that he would come for them. She left a note on the table for Daniel, took one last look around and turned and walked out. She would never return to this house again. Loretta looked back one last time as they drove away from her home. Home was where your heart was. Wasn't that how the saying went? And her heart belonged to Lorenzo. This was no longer her home.

Agnes drove her to her sister's place in Sawtell. "My sister Joan, will take care of you and her husband is a police officer. So you won't have to worry about Daniel trying to take you away. He will make sure of it."

Loretta could not thank her enough. She was a true friend. Agnes had been there for her the past nine years. Now she was finally free. She could make a life for herself and if anyone asked, she would say she was a widow. As far as she was concerned her husband was dead to her, and he would never see her or Rose again.

Daniel returned to the house late in the evening. It was dark and no fire had been lit.

"Loretta, Loretta, where are you? Why the hell is there no fire?" he yelled.

There was nothing but silence. He turned the light on. In the kitchen there was a note on the table.

Daniel
I have taken Rose and we have left. We will never return to you or this house. Do not come looking for us.

If you do, I will call the police and will have you arrested for assault. So to protect your good name it would be best for you to let us go. Loretta

It was dark when they arrived in Sawtell. Agnes pulled up outside a large cottage. There was a white wooden fence and gate which opened to a concrete path which led up to the front door. The lights were on and as they opened the gate a woman came out the front door.

"Oh Agnes, it's so good to see you Sis." The two women embraced. "This must be Loretta, I'm Joan." She put her arms around her and held her tightly. "You will be safe here. You will not have to worry about your husband again."

Loretta smiled the best she could. Her lip still hurt from where it had been split and it was painfully swollen. "Thank you."

"Now come inside and I'll show you where you and your gorgeous little girl will be staying." She placed her arm around her waist and led her inside. Agnes followed, carrying the sleeping Rose.

Joan led her through the house to a flat out the back of the house. It was small but homely. There was a large room which made up the kitchen, lounge and dining area, a bathroom and a large bedroom with a double bed.

"You can stay here as long as you need to. Our home is your home now."

Loretta looked at Joan. She had only just met this woman yet she felt safe.

"And you won't have to worry about Daniel. My husband is a police officer and he will pay him a visit tomorrow. He will make sure that he understands he is never to come near you or Rose again if he knows what's good for him."

Loretta cried. "How can I repay you, I have no money."

"That's okay. When you are feeling better and your bruises have healed, you can help me in my cafe by waiting at tables. I will pay you and you can help out around the house here and watch my kids from time to time. That is enough repayment for your board."

Loretta could not believe how lucky she was to have people who she had only just met be so kind to her. "Thank you. I can never thank you enough."

"Now get some sleep and we will talk in the morning." She kissed her cheek.

Agnes had put the sleeping Rose into bed already. She gave Loretta a hug. "It will be fine. You are safe now. Don't worry my sister and husband will watch out for you and if a letter comes from Lorenzo I will bring it straight to you. Now get some rest."

The two women left and went back to the house, Loretta climbed into bed beside Rose, not even bothering to undress. She was too tired and emotionally drained from the past twenty-four hour's events to care. She was finally free. She lay, simply enjoying the feel of the bed with the sheets somehow soft and crisp at the same time. Now at last she could sleep. She pulled the blankets up around her, trying to ignore the ache of her body, and closed her eyes. She was so tired. In the past twenty-four hours she had seen the best and worst of humanity. She smiled slightly, she knew which one would be with her the longest.

When Loretta awoke the next morning it took her a moment to realise where she was. The room was unfamiliar. Then it all came back to her. The savage beating, Agnes taking her and Rose away and coming to Joan's to stay. Rose was awake and on the floor beside the bed playing with some toys that Joan must have put in there for her. She looked up at her and jumped up on the bed wrapping her little arms around her mother's neck.

"Mummy are you sick?"

"Oh no baby. Mummy is fine. Mummy is really happy. We are safe now." She wasn't sure how much Rose would understand or remember as she was only three and a half. "We are going to stay here now. Just you and me. This is our new home."

Rose sat up and looked at her frowning.

"Daddy too?'

"No Rose. Not Daddy. Just you and me." Rose smiled and threw herself on top of her mother.

"Good. Daddy hurts Mummy. I'll kiss it better."

Loretta laughed. This child was a blessing from heaven and thankfully she had left when she did otherwise Rose may have been the next one that Daniel hurt.

"Come on. Let's see what there is to eat. Are you hungry?"

Rose nodded and jumped off the bed. In the kitchen the fridge was full of food. There was milk, eggs, fresh bread and fruit. Oh bless Joan, she had made sure that they could take care of themselves. After a breakfast of toast and jam and a cup of tea for her and a glass of milk for Rose they went up to the main house. She knocked on the door.

"Hello?"

"Come in Loretta dear. I'm in the kitchen."

It was very cosy and comfortable inside the kitchen. It was large, with a big wooden table and two seats either end and bench seats either side. Enough for eight people. There were pots hanging from the roof, bunches of garlic hanging beside the kitchen sink and a big wooden stove that had the most amazing smell coming from it. Outside the kitchen window she could see a vegetable garden.

"You look much better this morning. A good night's sleep did you well."

"Yes. Thank you so much. I don't know how I will ever be able to repay your kindness. After all, I am a stranger."

Joan placed her hand on Loretta's shoulder. "No dear. I have known for some time what you have been going through. Agnes asked me months ago if she could bring you here to stay if needed."

Loretta was stunned. "Really?"

"Yes. We have been putting a plan together for a while. Just in case you needed to leave in a hurry."

Loretta could feel the tears welling in her eyes. How lucky she was to have such beautiful, caring people in her life.

"Now, how about a cup of coffee?" She smiled and placed the kettle onto the stove to boil. "Then we will chat about what your new life is going to be like. One you are in control of, especially now you are a single Mum with a child to support."

Finally she would have a life of her own. One she would be in control of. Once she settled in she would write to Lorenzo to tell him where he could find her. Hopefully he would be able to come for them soon.

She missed him and he was missing so much of his daughter's growing years.

1st December 1948

Dearest Lorenzo

I have left Daniel and the farm, I'm now living in Sawtell with Agnes's sister Joan and her husband. Rose and I live in a little flat at the back of the main house. I have been working in Joan's cafe waiting tables and I am able to save a little money from my pay and tips.

Rose is well and is blossoming from all the love around her. She plays with Joan's children and is quite mischievous, just like her Dad. She resembles you more and more everyday. I miss you so much and long for the day that we can be together again. I have not heard from you for such a long time. Are you still coming back for us? Please write to me soon and let me know if and when you will return. The return address is on the back of the envelope.

All Our Love

Loretta and Rose xxxx

P.S. I have included a photo of Rose aged almost four.

It had been three months since she had left Daniel and the farm. He had not tried to contact her at all. Robert had gone back to the farm with Agnes to collect the rest of Loretta's belongings. He made it quite clear to Daniel that he was not to have any contact with Loretta or Rose. If he did it would become a police matter. Her father was not happy that she had left her marriage and had not spoken to her since. Loretta hoped with time that he would accept the fact that she would not return to Daniel.

She enjoyed her new life, but still missed Lorenzo. She hoped he would come for them soon. Her days now consisted of waiting tables and washing dishes in the cafe. She finally had money of her own and sometimes the customers would leave her tips. She loved her new found freedom. She helped Joan around the house with the cleaning, washing, ironing, helping with her kids and some afternoons they would walk to the park to play on the swings or throw a ball.

On the weekends they would go to the beach and swim. The weather was still warm and she loved the feel of the sand beneath her feet. The smell of the salty sea air and the sound of the waves crashing on the shore and the scream of seagulls overhead. Rose had so much fun building sandcastles, picking up seashells along the waterline and laughing at the crabs, running from them as they came closer.

She still had not had time to teach Rose to swim. She must make time, she thought to herself as they played in the little waves that came just up to her knees. If only Lorenzo was here. She was starting to lose hope that he was ever coming back for them. She stared out across the sea. In a strange way she felt closer to him here by the water even though he was so far away. She closed her eyes and said a silent prayer, hoping it would be answered soon.

CHAPTER 27

VERONA – ITALY

JUNE 1949

It had been over two years since he had received a letter from Loretta. He could not understand why she had not written back to him. Had she changed her mind? Did she not love him anymore? Was she okay? Maybe it was for the best. His mother would still not talk to him about the child or Loretta. She had forbidden it. The last time he had bought it up she had gotten herself so worked up that she had had chest pains and he had to call the doctor. He was not going to do that again. He could not risk it.

Paoletta came over at least once a week to chat and help him while he was working around the farm. They had gone out a few times to lunch or the movies but only as friends. She knew that his heart still belonged to Loretta and Rose. He was meeting her soon in town. They were going to have lunch, then wander through the markets. He washed up and changed his shirt and checked his mother was okay before leaving the house. He was worried about his mother as she had not been well for the last month.

Paoletta was waiting for him outside the cafe. It was a really quaint little cafe in one of the attractive medieval lanes. They served the best coffee in Verona and the food was divine. He waved as he approached. She smiled and waved back.

"Ciao Paoletta, it's good to see you. I hope I haven't kept you waiting too long?" He kissed both her cheeks.

"No I only just arrived, but I'm starving. Let's go eat. I'll need my energy for the markets."

He laughed. She did like wandering the markets, looking at all the handmade goods and jars of pickles and jams, and she could haggle with the best of them to make sure she got a fair price.

"Okay let's go. After you madam." He bowed and waved her past.

The cafe was busy and noisy with happy people enjoying the beauty of the day. They found themselves a table for two in the courtyard beside the fountain. The purple bougainvillea climbed up the wall and across the wooden trellis, the flowers so profuse that the wall looked like it had been painted purple. The table had a red and white check tablecloth, a bottle of water and two glasses on it. They took their seats and ordered coffee and a margherita pizza to share.

"Have you heard from Loretta yet?"

"No nothing. I'm sure she's getting my letters. I just don't understand why she has not written back."

Paoletta could see the hurt in his eyes. It made her sad. She had come to love him over the last two years. She knew he loved someone else but maybe if she waited long enough, he would realise that he would never be with Loretta and he would give up trying to bring her and the child here to be with him. Maybe, just maybe, the day he realised that, he would finally see her as a woman and a partner. Not just as a friend.

She made her voice quiet and persuasive. "I know you don't want to hear this but maybe she decided she didn't want to come to Italy and preferred her life in Australia."

"Well if that's true why hasn't she written to me and told me that? And what about Rose, my daughter? I can't bear the thought of not seeing her grow up. Seeing her walk for the first time, her first words, losing her first tooth, her first haircut. I have missed so much of her life already."

"I know but maybe it's for the best. You know your mother would never accept them. She would not even let them in the house if they came. I don't want to sound cold Lorenzo, but maybe it's time to let them go and move on with your life without them. Sometimes happiness can be staring you right in the face. You just have to open your eyes to see it." She fixed her gaze on him hoping he would finally see her.

Lorenzo knew she was right. It had been so long, and still no word from Loretta. Did that mean she had changed her mind? Maybe she had left Daniel. Maybe she had met someone else. He looked at Paoletta. He knew she was in love with him and he did care for her but not like he loved Loretta. He didn't know if he could ever love anyone like that again. Maybe it was time to let Loretta go. He was thirty three now. He needed to marry and start a family. He nodded, a tear ran down his face as he realised that maybe it was meant to be. He had to let them go. He would always hold them in his heart and never forget them.

They finished their meal, he pulled Paoletta's chair out for her and looked at her closely. She was a good friend and he did care for her. They walked back into the street to make their way to the markets. Past the 14th-century residence with its tiny balcony overlooking a courtyard known as Juliet's house made famous by Shakespeare's story of love and loss "Romeo and Juliet."

Verona was such a romantic, pretty town. The medieval cobbled streets, stone buildings with washing hanging between them, geraniums and bougainvilleas were flowering everywhere. Grandmothers were chatting to each other across balconies, little cafes had tables on the sidewalks with the smell of freshly ground coffee and food cooking.

There was so much history here. The old stone bridges, the Verona Arena, a huge 1st-century Roman amphitheatre built from local pink and white stone, the massive churches with their domes and cylindrical towers. It was so different to Australia he thought. Maybe he should try to go back and look for Loretta himself. But he could not afford the fare let alone leave his mother right now. She was not well and she needed him to take care of her. Maybe this was what his life was meant to be. Him here in Italy. Like his mother said, marry a good catholic girl. He reached for Paoletta's hand and held it as they walked around the markets. It's time to move on, he thought. Time to let go of the past and start a new future.

Paoletta smiled and chatted to just about everyone. It seemed like the whole town knew her. She was a pretty girl, well-educated and well-spoken. She finally knew he was letting Loretta go and now they could make plans to begin a new life together. She had waited patiently for him the past two years and he was finally seeing her as more than just a friend.

They purchased fresh vegetables and herbs from the vendors and some fresh flowers for his mother before leaving the markets. Lorenzo walked her to her car and bent and kissed her cheek.

"I will try to let them go. I know you have been patient with me these last few years. I can't promise you anything just yet. But I will try."

She smiled at him. "That's all I needed to hear Lorenzo. I will wait until you are ready. I've waited this long for you now, I can wait a bit longer. You know how I feel about you." He nodded, hugged her and kissed her cheek.

"I'll see you next week. I need some time to think." He turned and headed back down the cobbled streets to his car.

She watched him go and smiled to herself. Finally she would have her chance, to have a life and hopefully a family with Lorenzo.

Lorenzo placed the parcels from the market on the kitchen bench. "Hey Mama. I'm back, I've bought you some flowers." He placed them in a vase and took them into the lounge room. His mother was sitting in her favourite chair reading. She looked up as he came in and smiled. She was looking frail now. The death of his father had taken its toll on her.

"You are such a thoughtful son, thank you. There is a letter for you on the table. It looks like one you have written has been returned."

He looked at it. It was the last letter he had written to Loretta. It was marked Return to Sender not at this Address. His heart sank. He had no way of knowing if she ever received any of his letters. She must have left the farm and it was the only address he had for her. He had no way of contacting her now. How could he find her? Maybe she didn't want to be found. Maybe she had changed her mind and moved on with her life without him. Now he would never know. He looked at his mother. He wasn't sure if it was a look of sadness or "I told you so" on her face.

He needed space, fresh air and time to clear his head. He headed for his thinking spot under the old tree where he looked at his mountains. The ones he had described to Loretta so many times. As he sat thinking he realised this was a sign. It was time to let go and create a new life for himself without them. His heart was aching for what could have been and the child he may never see again. He had to accept the fact that his dream of bringing his family together would never be realised.

CHAPTER 28

SAWTELL

DECEMBER 1949

Loretta was cleaning the table after the last customers had left. A young couple very much in love, they had held hands the whole time they had sat there gazing into each other's eyes. She envied them. She remembered how Lorenzo used to look at her that way. It seemed so long ago. It was over three years since she had seen him. She still had the photos of him. One with her uncle and the other with Mathew and the horse and plough at the farm. They were getting tattered and worn by her constantly looking at them. She had not had a letter from him for so long and the real-isation that he was not coming back for them became more and more real everyday. She enjoyed her new life and freedom. She had money of her own now and new friends. She could go out whenever she wanted and Rose was thriving. She was always laughing and happy.

She finished cleaning the tables and washing the dishes. Joan had given her more work and responsi-bility. She would work the close up shift today so Joan could get to the school to watch her youngest in the school play. She heard the door open and looked at her watch. It was already five o'clock so who would be coming in now on closing time?

She called from the kitchen "I won't be a moment." She dried her hands and went to the counter. The man standing there was casually dressed. He wore shorts and a collared short sleeve shirt with the top two but-tons undone. He had a hat on which he took off as she came out. Underneath was a mass of thick blonde hair and a big broad smile.

"Sorry, I'm just closing up."

"Oh I don't need to eat. I just want to see if you would put this poster up in the window. It's for the dance next weekend at the town hall." He handed her the poster. "We are raising money for the Red Cross."

She glanced at the poster. "I'll check with the owner but it is for a good cause so I'm sure it will be fine."

He grinned, he had perfect white teeth, full lips and dimples in both cheeks. "My name is Martin" he held out his hand.

"Hello Martin, I'm Loretta." She shook his hand. It was warm and firm, she thought he was handsome and had such a calming voice.

"Will you be going to the dance?" He was still holding her hand.

"Oh probably not. I would need someone to care for my daughter." She pulled her hand away.

He looked disappointed. "Oh, you're married?"

"I'm a widow actually." It's not a lie she thought. Daniel is dead to me and he hadn't bothered me since the day she had left the farm.

"Sorry to hear that. Well if you change your mind I'll see you there, and maybe you could save me a dance?" He grinned and left before she could reply.

Loretta looked at the dance poster. How long since she had danced? She could not remember. Dancing around the kitchen with Rose didn't count. Why not go to the dance? It would be fun to mix with other people socially, and she did love to dance. Joan would watch Rose for her and she had money saved. She could buy herself a new dress to wear. It was about time she spoiled herself. She would ask Joan tomorrow morning. She finished locking up and headed for home.

"I would love to look after Rose for you dear. It will be great for you to get back out there and have some fun." Joan clapped her hands. "Oh what will you wear? Lets go shopping for a new dress for you. Robert's here. He can watch the kids while we go out. Grab your bag and I'll tell him where we are going."

She didn't give Loretta time to answer. Just headed off out the back calling to Robert "We're going out honey. Watch the children while we're gone, and no cordial for them either."

They drove into town, Sawtell was so pretty. The main street had tall trees planted in the centre that overhung and provided plenty of shade. They wandered from shop to shop trying to find that perfect dress. It was in Miss Patties shop that they came across a beautiful knee length dress. It was an aqua colour with a round neckline. Modest but not too modest, and made of silk with cap sleeves. It buttoned up at the back to fit her perfectly. Loretta looked at herself in the mirror. It had been a long time since she had worn anything so beautiful. If only Lorenzo could see me now. But he couldn't, and probably, would never see her again.

Joan could see her expression change. "You're thinking of him aren't you?"

Loretta turned and nodded.

"I know you still hope he will come for you dear. But it has been so long. It's been years since you have heard from him. Don't you think it's time to move on?"

Loretta knew deep in her heart he was not coming back, and she had to stop hoping he would return. It was only making her sad and lonely to keep daydreaming of the life that she thought she would have with him. It was only a dream. But today, was her reality.

"You're right Joan. It's time to let him go."

"Good girl. Now that dress is perfect. How about some new shoes to go with it."

They finished their purchase and headed back to the car Loretta could hear someone calling her name. It was Martin crossing the street coming towards them.

"Hello Loretta. It's good to see you again. Hello Joan." He tipped his hat to both ladies.

"Hello Martin. How is your father?" Joan asked.

"He's very well, thank you. Still out working and building houses. He won't listen to anyone about slowing down." He kept glancing at the packages in Loretta's hands. "Looks like you've been shopping ladies. Does that mean you are coming to the dance Friday night?"

Loretta laughed. "Yes, I'm coming to the dance Martin."

"Well remember you promised me a dance and I'll try not to tread on your toes too often. Afternoon ladies." He tipped his hat again, smiled and walked back across the road in the direction he had come from.

Joan turned to her "I didn't know that you knew Martin?" raising her eyebrow.

"I don't really. I only met him when he came into the cafe to put up a poster about the dance."

Joan chuckled and gave her a wink. "Well dear. I think he is sweet on you and I think he will want to dance with you all night. Now come on we'd better get home and save Robert from the kids. Hopefully they haven't tied him up to the chair." They both laughed and walked arm in arm to the car.

Loretta hung her new dress up in the wardrobe. It had been a long time since she had even thought of being with another man. She needed to finalise her life with Daniel before she could start fresh. She needed to get a divorce. She would go to see a solicitor tomorrow and start the process. Then she could finally be free to start a new life. One that she knew would not be with Lorenzo. It was time to let him go. She closed her eyes and could feel him beside her. You don't lose love like that, just because someone leaves. You only lose the chance to make new memories. Now it was time to start a new future making new memories.

"Goodbye Lorenzo."

The town hall was full of people, dancing and laughing, when Joan pulled up outside to drop her off.

"You will be fine. Go and have a good time." She patted her hand reassuringly and smiled. "Go on, off you go." She waved her hand at her to hop out of the car.

Loretta opened the car door being careful not to slip on the ground. It had been a long time since she had worn heels. She felt nervous as she walked up the stairs. She scanned the hall for someone she may know. She could see girls she worked with from the cafe. They were waving for her to join them.

"You look stunning Loretta. That dress is gorgeous. That colour really shows your beautiful hazel eyes." Peggy Lee was much shorter than her and was very curvy. She was always happy and loved a good gossip.

"Thank you Peggy Lee. You look very pretty too."

The girls were talking about all the single boys and who would dance with who. Loretta felt out of place, she was a few years older than the girls. She had already been married and had a child. She excused herself and went to get a drink.

On the counter there were tubs of ice filled with soft drinks and beer, tea urns and hot water for instant coffee. A large silver punch bowl was filled with lemonade, ginger ale, fresh lemon juice, sugar, ice cubes, crushed mint leaves and pineapple juice. Martin was pouring himself a glass when she approached. He was dressed in navy pants and a light blue collared shirt with a black tie. His blonde hair had been slicked back and he looked quite smart.

"Hello Martin."

The smile spread across his face when he saw her and his eyes had a definite twinkle in them now.

"I'm so pleased you came tonight. I didn't think you would seeing as I said I would probably tread on your toes when we danced. I thought it might have frightened you off."

She laughed. "Well, it could be the other way around. I haven't danced for a long time so maybe it will be me treading on your toes."

He handed her a glass of punch. She liked him, he had an honest face and there was something calming about him. He looked like he was the same age as her but she wasn't sure. She stood beside him and waited.

They were both nervous, unable to think of what to say.

"Are you going to ask me to dance, or stand there staring?"

He almost choked on his drink. He looked at her and chuckled. "Would you like to dance Loretta?"

"Sure. What have I got to lose except maybe my toes?"

He was quite a good dancer and for the next hour they danced and chatted. He was so easy to be with and she felt comfortable in his company. The band had played their last song and people were starting to leave.

"Well, I guess that's the end of the dance. Would you like to grab a coffee before you go home?" he smiled hopefully.

"I would love to." They walked across the road to the coffee shop that always stayed open on dance nights to catch last minute trade from the departing crowds on their way home after the dance. They grabbed a coffee and walked through the park finding a bench to sit on beside the pond. The ducks were

swimming around the reeds and a gentle breeze rus-
tled the leaves on the trees.

"You're not from here are you?" he asked.

"No. My family is from Dorrigo. Up the mountain." How much should she tell him? She wondered
that if she told him the truth would he not want to
see her again. Well it was better to have it all out in the
open now. She liked him and he deserved the truth.
"Martin I like you and I know you like me" he smiled
and nodded " But."

"Oh. Here it comes. The "But." His head lowered.

"No, I need to tell you something that could change
the way you think of me."

"You don't have to and I don't think anything you
could say would change how I feel."

"Yes I do, I'm ready to date again but I want to be
upfront with you."

"Okay, I'm listening." He leaned back on the seat
with his arm casually draped across the back waiting
for her to continue.

"I've been married before. Well, I still am actually.
I'm in the process of getting a divorce."

He looked at her steadily. "I thought you were a widow. That's what you told me."

She nodded. "That's what I've been telling everyone. The truth is my husband is dead to me. He was very abusive and he hurt me badly many times, for a very long time. We ran away after the last beating and I came here."

Martin didn't say anything. She wasn't sure if that was a good sign or not.

"It was an arranged marriage and he was much older than me. I never really loved him but I had to do as my father demanded. That's how it is in an Italian family."

"And your daughter is your husband's child?"

Well here goes nothing. She may as well tell him the whole truth. At least it would be out in the open.

"No. She isn't his." She lowered her eyes and she could feel herself starting to blush. She felt embarrassed by what she was about to say. She looked into Martin's eyes, she could not read what he was thinking. "During the war we had an Italian prisoner of war on our farm to help out with the farm work. We fell in love and Rose is the child of the love we shared.

He was sent back to Italy at the end of the war. He promised to come back for us but we have lost contact and I have not heard from him in a very long time."

Martin was silent for a moment then he smiled and took her hand. "Thank you for telling me. I like your honesty, and I do really like you Loretta. Your past is your past" he paused. "But are you ready to move on with someone else? Have you really left him behind in your past?"

Was she ready to let Lorenzo go and the dream of reuniting their family?

"Yes, I am Martin. It's time to let the past stay in the past. I want to have someone to share my life with."

He leant in and kissed her softly. His lips were so warm and delicious, pressed against hers. He tasted of coffee. Goosebumps rose on her arms and her heart raced faster. It was such a sweet, gentle kiss.

"Well, how about we take it slowly then and see where it takes us?' he grinned.

"I'd like that." She felt a flutter in her stomach. This felt right, and she was comfortable with her decision.

He laughed and hugged her closer to him. They sat and chatted for an hour before he took her home. He was such a gentleman. He walked her to her door, kissed her goodnight and left. She closed the door behind her and leant against it smiling. It was time to move on and start a new life.

CHAPTER 29

VERONA – ITALY
MAY 1950

Even though they had known each other for a couple of years, they had only really been courting for the last year and now today he was going to marry Paoletta. He stood at the altar. Beside him were his best man and groomsmen and the church was full of family and friends. There were large bouquets of white flowers everywhere and people chatting softly waiting for the bride to arrive. Lorenzo looked up at the large stained glass window in front of him. It was the image of Jesus on the cross with the light shining through sending coloured beams all around the altar. He knew he shouldn't be thinking of Loretta today. He was about to marry another woman but he could not help it. He still loved her. He would always keep her with him, deep in his heart and maybe one day Rose may come and look for him, her father. It would only be fair not to mention them to Paoletta again after today. She had been so kind and understanding all these years, but he was committing to her today as her husband and he did love her.

The pipe organ high up in the church balcony started the bridal march. The congregation stood for the bride to walk down the aisle. Lorenzo would have preferred a small wedding, but Paoletta was the only daughter and of course her father spared no expense. It looked like the whole of Verona had been invited. He turned as the two flower girls, his nieces, walked down the aisle hand in hand giggling and grinning, towards their uncle. They were followed by the three bridesmaids who were Paoletta's best friend and her cousins wearing pale pink long dresses with flowers in their hair. Then she appeared in the doorway. Lorenzo caught his breath. She was stunning, almost angelic.

Her dress had a fitted bodice with beading, tight fitting sleeves, a full skirt and a long lace train. Her father was beaming with pride as he walked her down the aisle to Lorenzo's side. He stopped beside him, turned and lifted her veil, kissed both cheeks and placed her hand in Lorenzo's.

"You take good care of my baby girl."

Lorenzo nodded. "I will. You have my word on it." And he meant it. Today was the start of a new life and he would make sure that he would never hurt her. He would be the best husband he could be.

He would never forget Loretta or Rose but this beautiful, caring, loving woman standing in front of him now, looking at him with so much love and hope deserved all his attention and devotion. He silently said goodbye to his Australian family and hoped that they were being loved and taken care of.

The service was a long, traditional Catholic wedding with all the readings and hymns. Finally they emerged from the church as husband and wife. The reception was being held at the family farm. It had been transformed with marquees and lights, long tables with white tablecloths, candles and flowers everywhere. A band was playing on the small portable stage in front of a wooden floor area which had been set up for dancing later. The men all gathered around the tent drinking the beer and grappa and laughing and joking, while the woman sat at the tables sipping wine as the children ran around playing and laughing.

Lorenzo looked around for his sister, catching her eye he gestured for her to follow him. They walked over to the bench under the tree and sat down.

"What's wrong Lorenzo?" Annettea was concerned for him. He seemed sad and happy all at the same time.

"Nothing Sis. Today is the start of my new life with my wife and I have decided I need to give her my full attention."

She knew what and who he was thinking of. She loved her brother and it hurt her to see him so sad. It had broken her heart to watch him trying to convince their mother to let him bring the Australian woman and child to Italy to be with him.

"I need to give you something in this box to keep for me. There are photos of Loretta and Rose, and letters I have kept. I don't know if Rose will ever come to Italy looking for me, her father. But if she does she may need them to prove who she is." A tear slid down his face. "I will never forget them but I must let them go for Paoletta's sake. We will never speak of them again. Can you keep them safe for me?"

She wrapped her arms around her brother's neck an she cried with him.

"Of course Lorenzo, I will keep them safe for you." She knew how devastating this was for him to let go of Loretta and Rose. He had held onto the dream for so long that he would be able to bring them to Italy to be with him. To be a family. It was hard for him to let them go. They held each other tightly for a moment then rejoined the party. Paoletta had watched the exchange between them. She knew what was happening.

He had told her a week ago that he would be putting the past to rest and committing himself to her and only her. It made her love him even more. She knew he would still think of Loretta and Rose from time to time and he would always love them, but now it was time to start their own family. Lorenzo was a man of his word and he had made his commitment to her today in front of their family and friends. He would not let her down.

CHAPTER 30

SAWTELL

DECEMBER 1950

Loretta looked at the signed divorce papers in her hands. Finally she was free from Daniel. It was official, it had not been easy. Loretta had to prove that there had been acts of cruelty towards her to be able to get the divorce. Luckily she had had the testimonies of Agnes and George. They had to appear in court and swear under oath. She had only seen Daniel once and that was at the courthouse for the final hearing. He did not even try to get custody of Rose. She could feel his eyes on her the whole time during the judge's decision. Even though she was shaking inside she did not make eye contact with him. She kept her head held high and stood tall and strong. She had made a new life for herself and Rose. She was now independent. She worked and had her own money, she had even saved enough for her own little car. It wasn't new but it was good enough for her.

It was only two weeks until Christmas now and she had almost finished all the present shopping with the help of Martin. He had been so good to her this last year. Rose absolutely adored him. He played with her all the time and when she heard his truck pull up outside she would run from the house laughing, calling his name. Even when they went out he always wanted her to come along. They still had plenty of time alone but he made sure that Rose was included and never felt left out.

She was falling in love with Martin more everyday. They had spent a lot of time together getting to know each other but taking it slowly. The three of them had gone out to the forest a week earlier, for a day's outing, to find a pine tree to cut down for their Christmas tree. Of course Rose had to pick the tree and it was so funny to watch them together marching through the trees with Rose barking orders at Martin to find the one that she thought was the best. She was five and a half now and had started school. She was clever and picked up things quickly but she had a mischievous side. They had bought Rose's chosen tree home on the back of Martin's truck and decorated it. Martin had lifted Rose up to put the angel that she had made at school on the top.

It reminded her of the Christmas she had shared with Lorenzo during the war when they had made decorations for their tree. She didn't think of him much now. He would always be the father of her daughter and she wondered if he ever thought of them. Had he moved on and started a new family of his own? She hoped he had. He deserved to be happy just as she was. She still loved him and always would but that was a lifetime ago. She had a new life now. One that included Martin. She loved him very much and she could see her future life with him. She knew he would always take care of her and love her and Rose. They had talked about a future together and now the divorce was final they could make plans.

Christmas Day had finally arrived and Martin was at their door early with his arms full of presents. Rose greeted him at the door in her pyjamas squealing with delight. "Hurry up Martin, Mum said we can't open the presents until you got here. Come on."

He laughed "Ok pumpkin. Let me put these down and give your mum a kiss. Then we will open them."

Rose started to collect her presents together. Martin grabbed Loretta and gave her a hug and kiss. "Merry Christmas beautiful."

"Merry Christmas to you too." She laughed and pulled away. "Now before this child bursts let's get these presents opened." They all sat on the floor, Rose looked at her mother, hardly able to control herself.

"Can I open mine now?" Rose cried out impatiently.

"Yes Rose. Open them." She was tearing the paper from the presents even before she had finished the sentence. There were new shoes and dresses, colouring pencils and sketch pads and a new doll with several dresses she could change the doll into.

They had decided to only give each other one present each. She had bought Martin a new watch. It was silver with a black leather band and she had it inscribed on the back with *Love Loretta and Rose*. Martin had bought her the beautiful aqua green cashmere cardigan she had admired at the shops a few weeks earlier. "To match your beautiful eyes," he told her.

"Mummy whose present is this?" Rose was holding a small square package, wrapped in gold paper with a bright red bow on top.

"That's for your Mum from me." Martin replied.

"But we agreed on only one present each Martin, I have nothing else for you."

"Yes, but this is a very special one from me to you. Open it."

Rose gave the box to her mother and looked at Martin and giggled. They shared a knowing look between each other as she hopped onto his lap.

"Oh. So you know about this Rose?"

Rose nodded. "It's a secret mum, I promised I wouldn't tell."

Loretta was impressed. For Rose to keep a secret would have been extremely hard. She took off the bow and unwrapped the box. She slowly lifted the lid and inside was the most exquisite ring she had ever seen.

It looked antique. It had a rose gold band, a solitary diamond in the centre and smaller diamonds on the side.

"Oh Martin." Tears filled her eyes as she looked up. He was on one bended knee in front of her.

"Will you marry me Loretta?"

"Say yes Mummy. Please say yes."

She looked back at the ring and started to cry. Could this really be happening? "Yes Martin, I will marry you."

Martin took the ring from the box and placed it on her ring finger and kissed her hand. He stood and pulled her into his arms.

"This ring was my grandmother's and I have been saving it for the woman that I want to spend the rest of my life with. And that's you. I promise I will love you and Rose for the rest of our lives. I will make you happy and give you the best I can. I love you Loretta. I have from the first day that I saw you, and I did ask Rose for permission to marry you first. I thought it was only right."

Rose sat there grinning. "He did mum and he made me swear that I wouldn't tell. I had to cross my heart too."

Loretta looked at the two of them and thought how lucky can I be to be so loved. "Kiss me, you fool. You can even say you love me if you like."

"I love you."

"I love you too"

They grinned at each other foolishly. Loretta stood on her tiptoes and flung her arms around his neck. The kiss he gave her was the softest, most gentle expression of love she'd ever experienced.

Rose danced around them clapping her hands in excitement, chanting. "We're going to get married."

CHAPTER 31

APRIL 1951

Loretta and Martin decided that they only wanted a small intimate wedding. They arrived at the court-house together with Rose. Already there waiting for them were Agnes, George, Joan, Robert and Martin's brother and his wife. Loretta wore a knee length cream linen dress with green edging. She had made it herself and on her feet were tan peep shoes. Loretta had also made a matching dress for Rose, their flower girl. She looked so sweet with a flower garland of daisies in her hair and carrying her small bouquet of roses. Martin wore a black suit with a cream tie made from the same material as her dress.

They stood holding hands in front of the judge facing each other. Rose was by Loretta's side.

"Martin, do you take Loretta to be your lawfully wedded wife, to love her, comfort her, honour and keep her, in sickness and in health, forsaking all others, as long as you both shall live?"

"I do."

"Loretta, do you take Martin to be your lawfully wedded husband, to love him, comfort him, honour and keep him, in sickness and in health, forsaking all others, as long as you both shall live?"

"I do."

"You may now exchange your vows."

"Loretta, I promise to love you and take care of you. I accept you with all your strengths and faults. I offer myself to you with all my strengths and faults. I promise you I will be a faithful loving companion and to always put the promises we made here today above all else." Martin squeezed her hand and smiled.

"Martin, I promise I will laugh with you in times of joy, and comfort you in times of sorrow. I will share your dreams, and support you. I look forward to starting our family together and spending the rest of my life with you. My best friend."

Martin placed the ring on Loretta's finger "With this ring I thee wed."

Loretta tried to place the ring on Martin's finger but it was too tight and she had to push it hard to get it on. Both burst into laughter. Finally "With this ring I thee wed."

The judge smiled "It is with great pleasure that I now pronounce you husband and wife. You may kiss your bride."

Martin took her in his arms and kissed her softly. Rose was squealing with excitement as everyone congratulated them. After the ceremony they went to Joan's cafe which she had closed for the day for the reception. Joan and Agnes had been busy the day before preparing food and decorating the cafe with flowers and balloons.

They enjoyed a lunchtime feast of cold chicken, ham, garden salad, pasta salad, Quiche Lorraine, fresh bread rolls with butter, beer and wine. The room was full of love and laughter. It was all they could ask for, surrounded by the people that they cared about the most.

Martin stood. "I'd like everyone to charge their glasses. I have a few words I would like to say to my beautiful wife and my beautiful daughter. I am the luckiest man alive to have you as my family. I promise you both I will love you always, I will protect you and take care of you, I will encourage you to be the best you can be, I will support you and your dreams to my very last breath. I promise you this in front of our dearest friends here today. Thank you for choosing me to be your life partner. I love you both dearly and I will for the rest of our lives."

Both Agnes and Joan were crying now and Loretta had tears rolling down her face. Loretta looked at this amazing, handsome man who was now her husband. She knew he would always be there for them and that he meant every word he had said. She knew that he would make her happy and that she could rely on him no matter what.

She raised her glass. "Thank you my darling husband. You have made me so happy and I promise I will take care of you forever." They clinked glasses.

"Besides you won't be able to get that ring off your finger now it's stuck there."

George raised his glass. "To Loretta and Martin."

Everyone raised their glasses and toasted the happy couple. "To Loretta and Martin."

Agnes had made her famous fruit cake and iced it white with little yellow flowers on top. There were figurines of a bride and groom, and a little girl. They cut the cake and moved to the area that they had cleared for dancing, for their first dance together as husband and wife they waltzed around the floor oblivious to everything else. Martin leant in and whispered in her ear.

"I will try not to tread on your toes. Come join us Rose." He scooped her up in one arm, his other around Loretta as they danced together.

"Martin?"

"Yes Rose."

"Can I call you Dad now?" He looked at the sweet innocent face and tears filled his eyes.

"Yes, I would like that very much Rose."

Loretta was also crying. Her life was so full of happiness and love for this man who loved her and her daughter. Her life was complete. They would have a few days alone together for a honeymoon in the local motel on the beach while Rose stayed with Joan, then they were packing up their belongings and moving to Maria River to work on a dairy farm. A new beginning and a new life together.

CHAPTER 32

The pains were coming hard and fast now. She had been in labour for six hours. She had gotten so much bigger with this pregnancy than when she was pregnant with Rose. She hoped the baby would come easily. It would surely be a big baby and it had been so active all the way through her pregnancy.

Martin had been by her side all day, encouraging her and holding her hand as she clenched it so tight when the pains hit. He thought she would break his fingers.

He wiped her brow with a cold damp cloth as she lay resting between contractions. She smiled up at him.

"Can I do anything for you?"

"I'd really like a banana split right now with chocolate topping and crushed nuts."

Martin threw his head back and laughed so much he had tears in his eyes. "You're giving birth and in pain and all you can think about is ice-cream?" They both broke into fits of laughter until the next contraction came.

Martin was sent out of the labour room to wait. She wanted him there but hospital rules did not allow the fathers to be present. Dr Grove's head popped up from under the sheet that covered her modestly.

"Okay Loretta. The head is crowning. It's time to push now with the next contraction." The pain came again hard and strong. She strained with every muscle pushing as hard as she could. The sweat was pouring from her brow. "That's good. The head is out. One more push and we will have a baby."

She had forgotten how painful childbirth had been. Only one more push and the pain would be gone and she would have a baby, their baby. The pain came again like a hot knife was cutting her from the inside. She pushed as hard as she could. Then the pain eased.

"It's a boy!" The doctor held him up for her to see. He had a shock of black hair and was screaming his head off. He was smaller than she thought he would be. The doctor handed him to the nurse to clean and weigh. He turned back to her just as another pain hit. He looked up at her in surprise. "Well Loretta looks like there's another baby on the way. You're having twins" he smiled. "There's a head crowning now, so give me another push."

Twins! Oh my god. That explained why she was so big and all the kicking. She pushed down hard again.

"It's a girl. Congratulations." She also had a shock of black hair. She was smaller than her brother but screamed even louder. "Well, she certainly has a good set of lungs on her." Dr Grove laughed.

"Let's get you tidied up first then I think we'd better get Martin in here to show him his new babies before he wears a hole in the corridor outside." Dr Grove smiled and gestured to the nurse to clean and wrap the babies.

Martin had been outside pacing up and down the corridor waiting for any news of Loretta and his first child. He didn't care if it was a boy or girl. As long as they were healthy. He wished he could have been there for her but the hospital would not allow him in the labour room. He had drunk so much coffee he didn't think he would sleep for a week. He heard a baby cry. He stopped pacing. Was that his baby? Still no one came out for him. A few minutes went by then another cry. What was going on in there? A nurse popped her head out grinning.

"You can come in now."

Finally he would get to see his newborn child. Martin was relieved to see Loretta. "Are you okay my love?"

She smiled. "More than okay, we have a boy!" The grin lit up his face "and a girl!" "What? What do you mean by a boy and a girl?" he was confused.

"Martin, we have twins." He took her face in his hands and kissed her.

"You are amazing Loretta, I don't know how I got so lucky." The nurse handed the babies to them.

"Congratulations, I'll give you a few minutes alone then Loretta needs some rest. You will be able to come back later to see her." She left them alone with their precious bundles.

Martin gazed down into the face of this beautiful child, his child. "Rose will be beside herself when we tell her she has a new brother and sister."

"Lucky we'd picked a girl and a boy's name? Hello Max and Daphne. Welcome to the family." She stroked Daphne's cheek softly.

"I'll let you rest darling. You need some sleep after that effort. I'll come back this evening with Rose to see you. I didn't think I could love you any more than I did, but right now Loretta I could just burst with how much love I have for you. You are my angel. I will treasure you forever." He kissed her forehead and left.

She lay back suddenly exhausted. She drifted off to sleep smiling. Life could not get any better than this.

CHAPTER 33

VERONA – ITALY

MARCH 1953

One by one the mourners had dwindled away after paying their respects to his mother. Lorenzo stood beside the grave, his shoulders slumped and a tear rolling down his face. Paoletta had already walked back to the car, with their two small children, to give him time to say a final goodbye to his mother. His mother had been ill for the last few years, finally dying in her sleep peacefully. He bent, and threw a handful of soil, a pebble clicked onto the coffin. He looked at the grave beside her. She was reunited with his father now. The wake was to be back at the farm. His sister would be staying overnight so they could clear their mother's things from the cottage that they had built for her beside the main house. Once he had married Paoletta she wanted them to have the main house. It had become too big for her, and she wanted them to have their own place to raise a family. He said his goodbyes, he didn't like cemeteries. It brought back memories of the war and his lost friends. It was time to go and have a drink and remember the good times and memories they shared.

The next morning they started the task of clearing the cottage. Their mother did not have a lot of things. She had been frugal all her life. It shouldn't take too long to pack them. They had to decide what they would like to keep for themselves as a reminder of her or to pass on to their children. The rest they would give to charity. Lorenzo was packing up the small kitchenette when Annettea came from the bedroom, she looked shocked and upset.

"What is it?"

She was carrying a small box. "I think you need to see this Lorenzo and I don't think you will like it either. It was at the top corner at the back of the wardrobe." She handed him the box.

Inside were several letters. He knew instantly they were from Loretta. He recognised her writing.

"What? What are these?" He pulled one out and started to read. He checked the others. They were all from Loretta. She had been writing to him. His mother had intercepted her letters and kept them from him.

"Mother did this to me? How could she?" He was shouting now. Anger and frustration of his mother's betrayal. "She kept her from me. How could she be so cruel and why keep them if she didn't want me to see them?" He could not believe this. He felt sick inside. He could feel a stabbing pain in his chest like his heart was being ripped in two.

"I don't know Lorenzo. I knew she didn't want her here but I did not think our mother would do something like this." Annettea was just as shocked as her brother.

"All this time I thought she had forgotten me, that she didn't want to come to me but she did. Look, this one says she left the farm. She had left Daniel. There is even a photo of Rose. My daughter at age four. She would be eight now." Annettea took the photo.

"She looks just like you. The same hazel eyes."

The pain in his chest was unbearable, he felt numb and empty. His hands were shaking as he wiped the sweat from his brow. He could not believe his mother had been so heartless. Lorenzo started to sob. He could've had a life with Loretta and Rose after all. She did still love him but because of his meddling mother it was not to be. He had a new life now with Paoletta and his children. He did love his wife but he cried for his lost love, Loretta.

They sat and read the letters together and Annettea cried with him. She knew how much Lorenzo had loved them both and still did, even though they never talked about Loretta and Rose.

"What will you do now Lorenzo?"

He thought for a moment. There was nothing he could do now. It was too late. They had both moved on with their lives.

"I will tell my wife what we have found. She has known about Loretta from the start. I know she will understand that I need to write to Loretta at the address she has given in Sawtell and hopefully she will receive this letter. I will explain to her what my mother did and to let her know that I never forgot her or Rose and I will be here if my daughter ever needs me. Paoletta knows I love her and our children, and she knows that they are my love and life now."

He stared at the photo of Rose. She was so much like him. What did she look like now? He wondered if she knew about him, that he was her father. Maybe Loretta had not told her. No matter what, he would write to her tonight and hopefully she would get this letter and know that he had never stopped loving her and their daughter.

Dear Loretta

I hope this letter finds you and Rose well. It is probably a shock to receive a letter from me after so many years. I must explain why. My mother passed away earlier this month and whilst clearing out her things, I came across your letters. She had kept them from me all these years. She would not accept the fact that I loved you and she had forbidden me to bring you to Italy. I tried to change her mind but she was very stubborn.

I had written to you many times. I do not know if you received them, I only had the farm address. Now I understand why you never got my letters. You had already left there. I want you to know I did try to save the money and convince my family to accept you both. But I gave up hope when I did not hear back from you.

I am married now and have two small children. We are living on the family farm in Verona. I am happy and my wife knows about you and our daughter. She also knows that I am writing to you and has given me her blessing. I hope you have found love and happiness also. I do not know if Rose knows about me? But if she ever needs me or wants to meet me, please let her know I will welcome her with open arms.

My warmest thoughts to you both.

Love Lorenzo xx

CHAPTER 34

MARIA RIVER

APRIL 1953

Loretta was surprised to see Joan drive up to the house. She wasn't expecting her, but then again someone was always popping in to help her with the twins. They were thirteen months old now and the line was always full of washing. They were a handful since they had started walking. Rose was a great help, but she was only eight. She never complained but she was still only a child herself. Before and after school Rose would help her with the chores and then play with the twins while she made the dinner. It was getting harder for her to get around now and they still had no electricity at the farm. She could no longer cut the wood for the stove. She was much larger with this pregnancy than the last one, and now that she was about to give birth to what they thought were another set of twins she needed all the help she could get.

"Come in Joan. I'm on the lounge. My feet are swollen again. I needed to put them up."

Joan came through the door, she was flustered and distracted. "I have a letter for you. I thought you might want to read it straight away." She paused looking down at the letter in her hand. She knew that this letter would upset Loretta. A letter from her past. A past long ago that she had left behind. "It's from Italy."

Loretta's breath seemed to leave her. A letter from Italy. There was only one person she knew in Italy and she had not heard from him for six years. She took the letter, her hands shaking.

"I'll make us a cup of tea while you read it." Joan disappeared into the kitchen. She knew Loretta would like to read the letter in private.

Loretta could hear Joan filling the kettle and gathering the cups. She was stunned. A letter from Italy. She looked at the letter again. It was Lorenzo's writing. She could feel her heart pounding. Why, after all these years, would he write to her now? Surely after all the years he wasn't coming back for them. It was too late now. She had found love again and had children with another man. A man she loved deeply.

Joan came back into the lounge room carrying a tray with the two mugs of hot tea and some biscuits, Loretta was sitting with the letter in her lap crying.

"Is it bad news dear?"

She handed Joan the letter. She could not speak. Unsure how she felt, she was still stunned and confused. Joan could feel the tears prickle her eyes as she finished reading the letter. She looked at Loretta and took her hand in hers unsure of what she was supposed to say. She knew how long Loretta had held out hope that Lorenzo would return for her one day. How hard it had been to let him go and move on with her life.

"So he did still love me. He did want to come for us. Now I understand why I didn't get his letters.

He didn't have my address after I left the farm. The letters must have gone there and Daniel would not have passed them on to me."

Joan said nothing. What could she say? She knew that Loretta had pined away for Lorenzo for years hoping that one day he would come back for them like he'd promised he would.

"He's happy and that's all that matters. He has a wife and children, just like I have my wonderful husband who I love and adore, and my beautiful children and the little ones on the way." She rubbed her big belly with affection. She smiled at Joan. "We are both where we need to be. We had our moment and it is just a memory. A beautiful memory."

"Will you ever tell Rose about her father?"

"I don't know Joan. Maybe when she's older, Martin is the only father she needs right now. He loves her like she is his own child. I will write back and let him know we are happy and doing well. I owe him that."

Martin has known about Lorenzo from the very start and she knew that he would support her with whatever decision she made when it was time to tell Rose about her father or to keep the secret.

Dear Lorenzo

I was very surprised and happy to receive your letter after so many years. I had waited for you for many years before I also finally gave up hope that you would return for us. At least now I know why I had not heard from you. It is good news that you are married and have children. I'm sure your wife is a very lovely woman. I have also remarried and have twins, thirteen months old and I am about to give birth again in the next month or so. The Doctor's think I'm having another set of twins.

My husband Martin is a loving, caring man and has been a great father to Rose. She is eight now and you would be very proud of her. She is doing well at school and is a happy, healthy child, and a great help to me with the babies. I have not told her about you as yet and I do not know when or if I will tell her. Maybe when she is older.

I know you would like to get to know your daughter, but at this stage I think it is best for Rose to keep this a secret. I will never forget the time we shared and I will cherish our memories. Give my regards to your wife and I wish you all well.

Love

Loretta and Rose

She finished the letter and placed it in the envelope along with a recent photo of Rose. At least now she could put the past to rest. Knowing that he had still loved her and Rose and had tried to come back for them. It had been fate that had kept them apart. She knew it would be the last contact she would have with Lorenzo. It was best to leave the past behind. A life together was never meant to be. She would not regret their time together. How could she? They had a beautiful child because of the love they had shared. She had a new life and family now. She didn't know if she could ever tell Rose about her father. She would deal with it when and if the time came.

CHAPTER 35

JANUARY 1959

Rose was seated on the small stool in the dairy milking the cow. In two months she would be fourteen. She liked life on the farm and with such a big family there was always lots of love and laughter. Max and Daphne were almost seven and inseparable. George and Charlie were five and always into trouble. They were starting school this year and Alice was three. She was such an angel with her blonde hair and cheeky smile, and she adored her big sister, following Rose everywhere.

The school holidays were almost over and soon it would be back to school for Rose. She had to be up early to make sure she had plenty of time to ride her pushbike the mile down to the ferry to cross the river, then ride another five miles to catch the bus into town to the high school. She didn't like school. The other girls teased her because of her olive skin and her clothes were second hand. She was a bright student and did well at all her schoolwork which made them tease her even more. Colleen, her best friend, always stuck up for her. She lived on the farm next door and they would ride their bikes to the bus together. Colleen was six months older than Rose, tall and thin, her skin sun kissed from years in the sun working. Her hair was red and frizzy, she had freckles on her face and the biggest laugh Rose had ever heard.

Colleen and Rose were inseparable in the holidays. Once they had finished their chores for the day they would meet up and go for a trip on the milk boat just for the fun of it. They'd ride their bikes down to the back plain before Christmas to pick the Christmas bell flowers. Her mother had shown them both how to sew on the Singer treadle machine. It took awhile to get used to the rocking of the feet on the pedal to keep the machine sewing continuously but once they did they made their own clothes. They got ideas from magazines and walking around the shops looking at the clothes, on the rare times they went to town.

Christmas Eve was the best. The family had finished the milking early so they could go to the carnival in town. It was their big treat for the year. They would have to line up for hours just to catch the ferry from Blackmans Point to Port Macquarie. It was the only way across and everyone went to the carnival. They were each allowed pocket money to spend on the rides or the sideshows and because Rose was older she was allowed to wander around with her friends, as long as she met Dad back at the front entrance at eight o'clock. They would leave earlier than everyone else so they didn't have such a wait at the ferry on the way back. Then off to bed as soon as they arrived home so Santa Claus could come and leave their presents.

Times were tough and they didn't have a lot, but her parents always put them first and they never went without. There was always lots of love to go around. They had a roof over their heads and food in their bellies. It had been hard the last five years with the twins being born so close together, and then Alice only two years later. Rose helped her mother a lot with the chores and tried to keep her brothers and sisters entertained so her mother could have some time to herself occasionally. The house was getting too small for all of them. It was only a three bedroom house. She shared a room with her two sisters. Her three brothers slept in the other bedroom. The other one for her parents. She would love to have some privacy, especially now she is fourteen, well almost fourteen.

Max and Daphne were expected to help now with the chores. Instead they were having a water fight out by the trough they were supposed to be filling for the calves. She could hear them laughing and splashing water, wetting each other. Then there was a loud splash and scream. She dropped the bucket spilling the milk and knocked over the stool as she jumped up to go see what had happened. Max was standing beside the trough and Daphne was in the trough totally soaked through. They were both laughing.

"What is going on you two?"

Max was laughing so hard he couldn't answer her.

"He pushed me in." Daphne screeched.

"No I didn't you fell in!"

Daphne splashed more water on Max then flicked some at Rose. Max joined her trying to wet Rose.

"Oh so you two want to play?" Rose took a step towards them grabbing the bucket they had been using to fill the trough and threw it over Max. He spluttered as the water hit him.

"That's not fair. Two against one."

The ground around them had become muddy, which made the game more fun. Rose slipped and landed in the mud. The twins squealed with delight. Max jumped on top of her now and Daphne joined in. The three of them were wrestling in the mud when Martin came around the corner to see what all the commotion was about. They hadn't heard their father approach.

"So this is what you kids call working then?" They all stopped abruptly and looked at their father.

"Sorry Dad. They started it. I was milking when I heard Daphne scream. I came to see what they were doing and they wet me."

He looked at the three children standing in front of him covered from head to toe in mud and started to laugh.

"Go on, get back to the house and clean up you lot, I'll finish the milking. Rose, see if your mother needs a hand. She's tidying up the store room so we can make a bedroom for you. Then you can have some privacy from these brats." He gestured to them to go.

"A room to myself. Really Dad? That's great." She went to cuddle him.

He put his hand up to stop her.

"Oh no you don't, I'd like to stay clean thank you."

Once she had washed all the mud from herself and the twins she found her mother in the store room. "Mum, am I really getting my own room?"

Loretta nodded. "Dad and I thought it was about time Rose. You are growing up so quickly and have started to blossom into a woman. It's best if you have some privacy. It's only the store room and small but once we clean it out and put up some curtains, add a bed and somewhere to put your clothes it will be cosy."

"Thanks Mum. I do love my sisters but."

"I know Rose. Come on let's sort through all this. I'm not even sure what's in some of these boxes."

They had three piles. One to keep, one to throw away and one to give to charity. There were old books, baby clothes, bassinet, empty jars of all sizes for jam and pickles, newspapers and magazines and lots of things they didn't need. Rose found a box of old photo albums. She opened one of them and thought she recognised some of the people and the place they were taken.

"Mum, who are these men in the photo?" Loretta took the album and sat on the floor beside her. She knew this day would come and Rose would have questions.

Loretta realised it was time to talk about the first four years of her childhood. Rose had never asked about her real father and Loretta wasn't about to bring it up. It bought back too many bad memories. Rose was no longer a child and she was old enough to understand. But how much should she tell her?

She pointed to a picture of Daniel, Lorenzo and her Uncle. "That is my Uncle and the man beside him is." She stopped, I can't tell her. I don't know how to tell her. What would she think of her mother? Rose was too young to remember the abuse she endured from Daniel and was she really old enough now to comprehend what had happened back then.

"Who is the other man?" She pointed to Lorenzo, she felt drawn to his handsome face. There was something about him that looked familiar to her but she could not figure out what it was.

"His name is Lorenzo. He was an Italian Prisoner of War and he was assigned to our farm during the war to help us. Every farm had a shortage of labourers as most of the young, fit men had signed up to fight in the war." No. She couldn't tell her the truth. Not yet, but she should know about Daniel.

"That man is Daniel, your father. You have always known that Martin was not your real father by birth."

"Yes I know Mum but he is the only father I know and he always will be my Dad." She paused and looked at the photo again. She didn't want to upset her parents, but she did want to know more about the man in the photo who was her father. "Is Daniel still alive?"

Loretta nodded. "I haven't spoken to him since the day we left the farm but Aunty Agnes still keeps in contact with him. He lives on the farm beside them."

"What about Lorenzo? Do you hear from him?"

Loretta looked back at the photo. She didn't know how to feel. It had been a long time since they had contact. I'm sorry Lorenzo she thought, I cannot tell her, not yet. "No, we lost contact years ago. He went back to his home in Verona, Italy after the war. He is married and has a family now."

Rose looked at the photo again. There was something about the Italian man, something familiar, but she couldn't quite work out what. "Mum, would you mind if I wrote to Daniel?"

Loretta shook her head. She knew this day would eventually come, if Rose wanted to get to know Daniel she would not stop her.

"I'll give you the address so you can write, but don't be disappointed if he doesn't write back to you. He has not tried to see you in ten years."

"That's okay Mum. At least I can say I tried" she hugged her mother. She could see sadness in her eyes. She knew there was something that she wasn't telling her, she had told her the truth, but not the whole truth, but she would let it be for now.

Dear Daniel,

My name is Rose, I am your daughter, I am fourteen years old and I know you have not seen me for ten years. I would like to get to know you if that is okay with you. I would also like to come to see your farm where I grew up. Could you please write back to me.

Your daughter Rose

CHAPTER 36

BELLINGEN

APRIL 1959

Daniel placed the letter on the table. He had read it several times. Rose, his daughter, wanted to meet him. It had been ten years since he had heard from Loretta or Rose. Life had been lonely since they had left, he had stayed on the farm and had decided that he was best to stay single. He knew Loretta had remarried and moved again and had more children. Here was a chance to see his daughter again to make up for all the things he had done to her mother and her. Daniel had had a lot of lonely years to think about the mistakes he had made and now was his chance to fix that. At least with his daughter. He knew Loretta would never forgive him for what he had done to her. He couldn't blame her either.

It had been arranged for Rose to stay with Agnes and to spend the day with Daniel but Loretta had forbidden her to stay overnight at her father's farm. She would not tell Rose why.

Daniel stood on the veranda watching as the car drove slowly down the driveway. They pulled up at the gate leading to the house. He could see Agnes behind the wheel and a young woman beside her. He carefully walked down the steps using his cane. His leg had given him a lot of trouble over the years, and now he had to use his walking stick all the time.

Rose watched him as he made his way down the stairs. She didn't realise that he would be so old. Then again, she did remember that her mother had told her that it had been an arranged marriage and he was much older than her. What would she call him? Martin was the only father she knew. She would not call him Dad, Mr Bridges was too formal so she would just call him Daniel. She felt nervous as she stepped from the car.

"Hello Agnes."

"Hello Daniel. This is Rose." She put her arm protectively around her. "Rose, this is Daniel."

Rose politely took his hand and shook it. "Hello."

"Hello." He smiled. Not sure of what to say next, there was a moment of awkward silence. "How about I make us all a cup of tea? Please, follow me inside." He shuffled back up the stairs. Agnes took her hand and gave it a reassuring squeeze.

They followed him into the house. It was small, dark and it had a musty smell, but it seemed vaguely familiar to her. *So this is where I spent the first four years of my life?* There were photos on three of the walls. A man in an old hat on a horse, an old photo of a bride and groom, a woman holding a baby which she presumed must be her and her mother, two young men standing in front of a barn, a waterfall and one of a man in uniform. Also a very old photo. It was faded and had creases in it. The other wall had been painted white and was bare. Daniel came in with the pot of tea, three cups, milk and sugar.

"Sorry I only have store bought biscuits. I'm not one for baking cakes. Please sit down." He placed the tea and biscuits on the table.

Rose wondered what do I say to this man. How do I start? Agnes poured the tea, she could feel how uncomfortable they both felt.

"Tell Rose about your photography Daniel." Agnes didn't like Daniel. She had tolerated him all of these years, but she knew what he had done to her friend and she would never forgive him for that. But for Rose's sake she would be friendly.

For the next hour he told her of how he had come to love taking photos in the mountains and forests around the area. Of the scenery and wildlife and what times were best to take photos. He explained that the blank white wall behind her was for his projector to show the slides he had taken. Agnes looked at her watch.

"I have to go, but I'll be back at five o'clock to pick you up Rose."

Daniel stood and cleared the cups and teapot from the table. "I'll put these in the sink and then I'll take you for a walk about the farm."

Agnes gave her a cuddle. "If you need me to come back earlier or if anything happens just call and I will be straight over."

Rose wasn't sure why Agnes was so worried. What hadn't they told her about Daniel?

"I'll be fine Aunty Agnes, I'll see you at five."

They chatted as they strolled down to the creek. It had taken them a while as Daniel could only walk slowly on the rough ground with his walking stick. There were tufts of grass and sticks laying across it that may have tripped him. The track looked like it had not been used in a long time. The creek was so beautiful with the little rapids, the sound of the water cascading down the rocks and into the pool. Then winding its way down around the bend. There was a little sandy area just like a little beach and there were so many butterflies flying around in the sunlight that filtered through the trees. She remembered this place. She had been here before.

"Your mother used to bring you down here all the time when you were little. You would chase the butterflies trying to catch them." He smiled at her. She had grown up to be a very beautiful young woman.

No thanks to me he thought. Loretta had done a fine job.

"Would you like to come back to the house and I will show you some of my photos and slides?"

She nodded. "Yes I would like to see your photos, especially the landscape and animals."

They spent the rest of the afternoon in the lounge room with the curtains drawn to make it dark enough to view the slides. He was a very good photographer she thought. Maybe if I come back I might get him to teach me how to take photos.

Agnes arrived right at five o'clock. They said their goodbyes and Daniel gave Rose an awkward hug.

"I hope you will come back and visit me again soon Rose. I have really enjoyed getting to know you again after all these years."

Rose had enjoyed herself and it had been nice to see where she had lived as a small child. She didn't feel any love for this man even though he was her father, but she did like him. Maybe if she gave it more time love would grow.

"Yes I'd like to visit again, and thank you for a lovely day." She kissed his cheek and hopped into the car.

Daniel watched her drive away. He could feel the tears rolling down his face. He may not deserve a second chance with his daughter, but she was willing to give him one. So he would make sure that he would not disappoint her.

CHAPTER 37

MARIA RIVER

MARCH 1960

Rose enjoyed her job pulling the ferry across the river on the weekends. There was a big steel drum with a groove in it in which the steel rope sat. The rope then went from one side of the river to the other over that wheel. She had to turn the handle to work the ferry across. It gave her pocket money to spend on herself. It was hard work winding the handle to drag the ferry across the river, but it also gave her a chance to meet and chat to people. She never seemed to have much time to herself in between school, chores on the farm and helping with her younger siblings. She was fifteen now and very mature for her age.

She had been to visit Daniel on his farm in Gleniffer a few times now. Only for a day visit as her mother still would not let her stay overnight with him. She would catch the bus up to Bellingen and Aunty Agnes would pick her up and drop her to Daniel's. She liked taking the bus. It took half a day to get there by the time they made all the stops to pick up and drop off passengers along the way. It was fun to watch the people on the bus and wonder about their lives. Aunty Agnes and Uncle George were fun to stay with, she knew they weren't her family by blood but they had always been there for her and her mother. It was the only time she had to herself without her brothers and sisters. She savoured every minute of it.

Rose was sitting under the tree by the river waiting for the next load of cars and people to pull across to the other side. Sunday was usually busier than Saturday as a lot of people went to church and the kids went to Sunday school. A car drove down and pulled up beside her. There were four young men inside. She had seen three of them around before but not the other one. He was tall with dark brown hair and the bluest eyes she had ever seen. She could see the hair on his chest poking out the top of his short sleeve shirt. He had left the top few buttons undone, his arms were muscly and he was tanned. Probably from working in the sun all day.

He caught her eyes and she realising she had been staring. She could feel the colour rise in her cheeks as she blushed. He was walking towards her now.

"Hi, my names Jimmy"

"Hello, I'm Rose"

"Hard work for a girl working the ferry. That's impressive." He smiled.

She could see his perfect white teeth and those eyes were so blue. She felt a tingle at the back of her neck.

"It's not so bad once you get used to it."

"So you live around here Rose?"

"Yes our farm is a mile back that way." She pointed across the river. "How about you?"

"My family owns the dairy farm on this side of the river, I work it with my parents and brothers and sisters."

They were on the other side by now and his friends were calling him to hurry up.

"Well I have to go, I hope I see you again soon Rose." He winked at her and joined his friends. Rose was smitten. He was so handsome she was sure she would see him again.

Every weekend for the next month Jimmy crossed the river every Sunday. He would always talk to her. She knew he liked her and she liked him. Every time she saw him she got butterflies in her stomach. Today he asked her if she would like to go to the dance next Saturday night at the community hall. She hoped her parents would let her go, she was fifteen now and all the other girls her age had been allowed to go dances with a boy.

"Yes you can go Rose, but I will drop you there and pick you up."

"But Dad I'm fifteen now, I'm a woman."

"No Rose. You are a young woman, and he is three years older than you. You can go out but only if I drive you there and pick you up."

Rose knew it was no good arguing with her father. At least she could go to the dance and meet Jimmy.

Just wait till all her friends saw her with her date for the night. They would be so jealous.

"Okay Dad" she hugged him and kissed his cheek "You're the best Dad ever!" He laughed and squeezed her.

"Yes I am, but this boy better behave himself with my girl, or else." He wagged his finger at her, giving her his tough look face.

Her mother had taught her to sew years ago and now she helped her modify one of her old dresses to wear to the dance. It was aqua green silk.

"I wore this dress to the dance the night I met your father Martin. I had the best night that night. We danced so much my feet hurt and that was not from him treading on my toes." They both laughed. They took the hem up so it was just above her knees and took it in at the waist. Rose put it on and looked in the mirror. It was beautiful.

"You will turn everyone's head at the dance, I think you will have all the boys lining up to dance with you." Loretta had tears in her eyes looking at her daughter. She was so beautiful. When had she grown up so much? It only seemed like yesterday they were placing a baby in her arms.

The week seemed to drag on for Rose, between chores on the farm and schoolwork. Finally it was Saturday night and her father was opening the car door for her outside the hall.

"Now have a good time and make sure you don't leave the hall or your friends. I'll be back at ten o'clock sharp to pick you up."

"I will. I promise Dad." She gave him a kiss and ran inside to find her friends. The girls were all in a group on one side of the hall waiting to be asked to dance, while the boys stood on the other side of the hall. Then she saw him. He looked so handsome in his jeans and white shirt with the long sleeves rolled up to his elbows. His dark hair was slicked back, his eyes twinkling, as he approached her and smiled. All the girls started chattering, thinking that he was coming over to pick them for a dance. He held his hand out to Rose.

"Can I have this dance?"

She shot a look of satisfaction at her friends. They were so envious.

"Yes you may." She took his hand and he led her onto the floor for the barn dance.

The night went so quickly. Jimmy had stayed by her side all night. They danced and talked but soon it was time to go. It was almost ten o'clock. He took her hand and walked her outside to wait for her father.

"I'd like to see you again Rose." He reached out and touched her cheek. It sent a prickle through her skin.

"I'd like that too." He gave her a gentle kiss on the lips. It felt like a jolt of electricity going through her body.

"I thought I'd better do that before your Dad gets here, I don't think he would like me kissing his daughter in front of him."

She giggled. "No, probably not, he would more than likely punch you."

They held hands until Martin arrived. She introduced him to her father then got into the passenger seat. Martin said a few words to Jimmy, they shook hands and he hopped into the driver's seat.

"What did you talk about Dad?" She hoped her father hadn't said anything to embarrass her.

"He asked if it would be okay if he came around the farm to see you sometimes. I said it would be all right. I invited him for dinner next Sunday night so your Mum can meet him."

Rose smiled. He was coming for dinner. She just hoped that her siblings would behave and not make a fool of her in front of him.

CHAPTER 38

APRIL 1960

Rose checked her dress for the third time. She had tried on several dresses, trying to find the perfect one for tonight's dinner. Finally she chose the blue, knee length one with the sweetheart neckline and cap sleeves. Jimmy was coming for dinner tonight to meet her parents and brothers and sisters. She hoped that they would not make a fool of her in front of him. She kept thinking of the kiss outside the dance a week ago. The thought of his lips on hers sent a shiver down her spine. It had been so soft and gentle.

Closing her eyes, she transported herself back to the moment their lips touched for the first time, his tender embrace and the sensation of his hand resting around her waist. She had never experienced feelings like this before.

As she entered the kitchen she could smell the lamb roast and baked vegetables wafting through the door. Max and Daphne were laughing and chasing each other around the table.

"Will you two stop it and make sure you behave and please don't say anything silly tonight to embarrass me in front of Jimmy."

"Oh come on Sis. Like I would do that." Max laughed.

"I mean it. I really like him. If you do anything to humiliate me I will hit you so hard." Rose held her clenched fist up to Max shaking it.

"Rose, that's enough. They will behave tonight." Loretta gave them both a stern look. "Or they will be grounded and both will have to do the washing up for two weeks with no help. Understand?"

Max and Daphne stopped running and replied in unison "Yes Mum."

Loretta returned to cutting the roast. "Now outside you two until I call you for dinner." They scuttled outside still laughing. The gravy was warming on the stove top and the trifle and custard for dessert was in the fridge. Rose looked at her mother and smiled.

She loved her so much. She was lucky to be her daughter. They had spent many hours together. Loretta showing her how to sew and cook. She was never too busy to sit and talk to her about things that bothered her. About school and her friends, even though there were so many of them in the house. Her mother always put everyone else first no matter what and her parents were still so much in love. She hoped she would have a love like theirs.

Her father came into the kitchen, went straight over to Loretta and patted her on the bottom. "Mmmm that smells good beautiful." He kissed her neck gently. "I don't know what I did to get so lucky to have you as my wife?"

Loretta turned and smiled at him. "I'm the lucky one. Now get out of here before I burn the gravy.' She made a swipe at him with the tea towel as he left the kitchen grinning. There was a knock at the door.

"I'll get it. That will be Jimmy."

Rose raced through the kitchen up the hall to the door. She opened it to see Jimmy standing there dressed in jeans and a yellow checked collared shirt. He was so handsome with his short dark hair slicked back. His square jaw was clean shaven. It made her melt. He had a bunch of flowers in his hand.

"Hello Rose."

"Hi Jimmy." She heard her voice falter and she was so nervous. "Come in." He followed her into the kitchen. "Mum, this is Jimmy."

Loretta put the pan down and wiped her hands on her apron. "Hello Jimmy. It's so nice to finally meet you. We've heard a lot about you."

"It's very nice to meet you." Jimmy held out the flowers. "These are for you. They are from my mum's garden."

"Thank you. They are lovely. Rose, grab me a vase please and put them on the dining table. Martin is in the lounge room. You two go in there and join him while I finish up here. I'll be there in a minute."

Rose took the flowers and placed them into a vase with water and an aspirin. Her mother had shown her that flowers lasted longer and fresher if an aspirin was dissolved in the water.

Jimmy followed her into the lounge room which was also the dining room. The table had already been set for dinner. Martin was seated in his favourite armchair. It was an old navy chair and the arms were worn in places. Her mother wanted to get a new one but he wouldn't have a bar of it. He would laugh and say, "I hope you don't want to trade me in on something new when I get old and worn out."

"It's good to see you again Jimmy. Please have a seat."

Jimmy sat down on the lounge and Rose sat next to him. Close but not so close that would upset her father.

"So Jimmy. Tell me. What do you do for work?"

"Well Sir, I work on the family dairy farm. I help with the milking and ploughing the fields for the corn and turnip crops. It's an early start each day as you know. I love the land. Especially driving the tractors and ploughing the fields for the crops."

Martin nodded. "Call me Martin. Yes I do enjoy that myself. Nothing like the smell of fresh dirt turned over. Do you have brothers and sisters?"

"Yes. I have five sisters and a brother. I did have another brother but he passed away eight years ago when I was ten." A sadness passed over his eyes.

"I'm sorry to hear that. So a big family like ours. This house is always filled with love and laughter. Just like yours I imagine?"

Jimmy smiled. "Yes and my older sisters are like mother hens. Always brooding around me. We all help out on the farm."

Loretta entered the room. "Dinner will be served in five minutes. Rose, can you round up your brothers and sisters and get them to wash up for dinner please."

Rose excused herself. She found them all out the back playing with the dog. "Come on you lot. It's time to wash up for tea and remember to behave yourselves. No silly talk at the dinner table please."

Max stuck his tongue out at her cheekily. "Rose has got a boyfriend, Rose has got a boyfriend," he chanted.

She laughed and gave him a gentle smack to the back of his head as she ushered them all to the bathroom to wash their hands for dinner. She helped Alice to wash her face and hands and straightened their clothes, she wanted to make a good impression on Jimmy.

When they entered the dining room Jimmy and Martin were already seated at the table and her mother was placing the last of the plates down. Jimmy stood to pull her chair out for her to sit. She blushed. No one had ever done that for her before.

They enjoyed polite conversation over dinner and everyone was on their best behaviour. Even Max was polite although a little bit shy. Once they had finished she helped her mother take the dishes to the kitchen while Martin and Jimmy went out to the back veranda to talk about farming.

"Well Mum. What do you think of Jimmy?" Rose looked at her mother hopefully. She needed her to like him.

"He seems like a nice young man, but remember you are only fifteen and he is eighteen. So take your time and don't rush into anything or feel like you are forced into doing something you are not comfortable

with. He is your first boyfriend and do not put yourself in a position that it will lead to anything more
than a kiss. You know what happens if you go too
far?" Loretta was looking at her intensely now, with
motherly concern in her eyes.

"I know Mum. I promise I won't. But he's so handsome isn't he?" she gushed.

Loretta chuckled. "Yes he is Rose."

They finished cleaning and joined the men on the
veranda. The sun had set over the river and the last
golden rays were disappearing on the horizon. The
clouds still had a slight tinge of pink and mauve that
slowly faded to grey with the setting sun. The cows
were settling down for the night and the only sound
in the stillness of the last rays of daylight were the birds
calling in the trees.

Martin nudged Loretta and gave her a wink. "Well,
we will be going inside to listen to the news on the
radio. We'll let you two chat for a while. Not too long
though Rose. You have school tomorrow."

"Yes dad I know." She smiled to herself. At last she
would be alone with Jimmy. She moved closer to him.
He put his arm around her shoulders and pulled her

closer. She could feel the warmth of his body and the delicious scent of his aftershave. He placed a finger under her chin and lifted her face to him, their eyes connected. He had such long, thick lashes and he smiled.

"I think your family like me. I really like you a lot Rose. Would you be my girlfriend?" His blue eyes had a twinkle in them and his smile made her all fluttery inside.

She laughed nervously. "Oh Jimmy I would like that more than anything."

He pulled her closer and kissed her softly on the lips. They sat and chatted for a while longer, making plans to meet again the following weekend.

"Rose. It's time to say goodnight." Her father was standing at the door. "Nice to see you again Jimmy."

"Okay Dad. I'll just walk Jimmy to his car and I'll be in."

"Thank you for a lovely dinner Sir, I mean Martin and please thank Loretta for me and tell her Goodnight."

"I will. Don't be long Rose."

They walked around the side path to where Jimmy had parked his car. The pathway was dimly lit and uneven. Rose tripped and stumbled. Jimmy reached out to steady her.

"Well looks like you've really fallen for me then doesn't it?" Jimmy laughed.

Rose could feel her cheeks burning. How embarrassing to trip over in front of him but she could see the funny side and laughed with him. He kissed her goodnight and drove off down the dirt road heading for the ferry and home.

Loretta and Martin were sitting in the lounge room when she entered.

"Well, he seems like a fine young man Rose. He's polite and respectful and a hard worker too. But remember you are only fifteen and he is eighteen. So you take it slowly. No rushing into anything. Remember you have a bright future ahead of you and you don't want to go tying yourself down to a boy. There's plenty of time for that later on." Martin's tone was of concern and love for her. She knew he was looking out for her.

"Yes dad I know. I promise I will take it slowly." She gave them both a kiss. "Thank you for tonight. I love you both so much."

"We love you too darling. Now off to bed." Loretta patted her on the cheek and smiled. Her little girl was growing up so fast.

As Rose crawled in between the sheets she smiled. She had a boyfriend. She closed her eyes, she could still feel his warmth and the smell of him, the way he looked at her and the way he made her feel. She was so happy her life was so good right now. Wait until she arrived at school tomorrow and told her friends. They would be so jealous.

CHAPTER 39

OCTOBER 1960

The last six months had flown by, with school, chores at home and on the farm and every chance she had to spend with Jimmy. They saw each other most weekends and sometimes after school. He would wait for her at the road as she rode past his farm on her way home. Today as she rounded the bend on her push bike there he was, leaning on the old gate post waiting for her. The smile spread across his face as he saw her. Rose felt a thrill of excitement on seeing him there waiting for her. He'd obviously been in the dairy working. His hair was messy, he had mud on his boots, his arms were glistening from sweat and there was a smudge of dirt on his cheek where he had wiped his hand across his face.

Rose pulled up beside him and jumped off her bike, dropping it on the side of the road. He grabbed her around the waist and picked her up to give her a kiss.

"Hello beautiful. How was school today?"

She hated talking about school with him. It made her feel like a child. She would be sixteen in another six months.

"It was fine. We received our results today and I've topped the class in English and Maths. I've been accepted into a government course next year. But it's in Canberra." She looked down at her feet. She wanted so badly to do the course but that meant leaving Jimmy. She had worked so hard to make sure she was accepted for the course and it was a great achievement.

Jimmy could sense her anguish. He pulled her closer. "That's fantastic Rose. Don't worry I'll be here when you come home for the holidays. I might even be able to come down to visit." He placed his hand under her chin and lifted her face so he could look into her eyes. There was a sadness there that shadowed her usually normal cheerful demeanour. He kissed both cheeks then her lips.

"Come on, smile. You're too pretty to frown. Besides, it will give you wrinkles." She elbowed him in the ribs and laughed.

"I have to go out to Dulhunty Island on Saturday to check the yard and fences before they put the cattle back out there. Would you like to come with me?"

Rose's eyes lit up. "Oh that would be great, I'd love to. I will pack some lunch to take with us."

"Okay then. We will leave at ten on Saturday morning. I will pick you up from the ferry and we will row across from the milk wharf. I've got the boat already there. You'd better get going otherwise you will be late getting home." He gave her a quick kiss and hug before she jumped on her bike and headed for the ferry.

On Saturday morning she met Jimmy at the ferry. She wore her cute little shorts with a red check button up top with cap sleeves. Once she had ridden away from the house and out of her parents sight she had undone enough buttons to show a bit of cleavage, but not too much. She had her sand shoes on and her hair pulled back into a ponytail. Jimmy was leaning against the car waiting for her. He smiled and tilted his head to one side. His eyes glinted with mischief. He opened the car door for her with a flourish.

"Your chariot awaits madam."

She giggled and slipped into the front seat. He placed her basket with the food and blanket in the back seat. She liked this car. It had a bench seat in the front so she could sit beside him, nice and close.

They pulled up beside the wharf where the milk boat pulled in to collect the milk cans from the dairy. He helped her into the boat, untied the rope holding it to the wharf and gave it a push as he jumped in. The island sat in the middle of the river. It was about forty acres in size. Normally there would be cattle grazing on the island but they had all been taken to market a few months ago. Jimmy now had to check to make sure all the fences and yards were in good condition before the next load of cattle were sent out to graze here. There was also a small shack on the island that was used for storage and sometimes the local boys would go out there and camp overnight. Or go fishing.

Rose watched him as he rowed the boat. He had such a muscular physique with his broad shoulders and dark hair glistening in the sun. His muscles rippled as he pulled the oars back and forth, gliding them across the water to the small sandy beach where they would tie the boat up to a log. Clouds had started to roll in from the east and the wind had come up as they rowed across the river.

"Let's put these up in the shed. Just in case it rains." Jimmy grabbed the food and rug from the boat. "Looks like it will only be a passing shower. We should be right."

They took the food and rug up to the shed. Then they set off to walk around the island checking the fence and gates. The land had mostly been cleared, except for around the edges where the bloodwood trees and gum trees still stood offering shade to the cows in the heat of the day. Everything was in good order so they had plenty of time to sit down and relax and talk. They spread the blanket out underneath the old gum tree. It was warm and the clouds were building up now. They finished their food and lay back on the blanket, gazing at the clouds, both lost in thought.

"Rose, it's selfish of me but I don't want you to go away next year to Canberra. I've fallen in love with you and I don't want us to be apart."

Rose rolled onto her stomach and placed her head and hand across his chest.

"I know. I love you too. I don't want to go either, but I have promised my parents that I will follow through with the course. They are so proud of me and have done so much to get me where I am today. I can't let them down." Her eyebrows furrowed, a small crease formed above her nose and she bit her lip. "You won't forget me and find someone else when I go will you?" She had tears in her eyes. She couldn't bear the thought of leaving him but she knew she had to do it for herself and her family.

"Don't be ridiculous. There is no one else for me. You are the one I want to be with." He moved closer to her and his mouth was deliciously close to hers. His warm breath grazed her skin. Leaning in, he paused then placed his lips on hers. Her skin ached for his touch, he rolled her over onto her back. The weight of his body gently pinned her against the blanket as they engaged in a hot, fiery kiss.

Every inch of her body wanted to feel his touch, his love. Wrapping her arms around him, she closed her eyes, lost in the luscious moment and shutting out the world around them. Just then the skies opened above them and the rain came down with such force they were wet within seconds. It was only a sun shower but enough to drench them.

They jumped up and raced inside the old shed to get away from the rain. Through the thin fabric of her now wet top he could see the outline of her nipples and had to brace himself as lust hit him like a hammer. They drank each other in with their eyes. They were both smiling, breathless, laughing at the craziness of the weather. The laughter faded and they moved together, reaching out, his hands cupping her face, her fists closed around handfuls of his shirt as their mouths met and their bodies came together.

Leaving a trail of kisses on her neck, he whispered in her ear.

"Will you marry me?"

Rose was stunned. Had she just heard him right? She pulled back from him. She looked into his eyes, sparks shivered along her nerves, her heart was pounding.

"What did you say?"

"Will you marry me Rose? I know you're only fifteen but we can wait until you're sixteen and I'm sure your parents will give their blessing."

Rose was beside herself with joy. He wanted to marry her.

"Of course I will marry you."

She placed her hands on either side of his face and stood on her tiptoes, pressing her lips against his.

His body quivered under her touch and he pulled her against him, his warm, muscular frame making her knees weak making her heart pound. Pushing her gently against a wall, Jimmy nuzzled her neck and savoured each hot, blissful kiss. He gently unbuttoned her shirt, slowly running his fingers over her shoulder. Trailing his hand down her body, he reached behind and undid her bra strap at the back with ease. As he slid it off she let out a low moan.

Rose slid her hand under his shirt, her fingers feeling the curly chest hair, his skin was warm and damp.

She unbuttoned his shirt and pushed it back over his shoulders stepping back to look at him. Her hands moved slowly over his hairy chest. The hairs on her arm were standing on end. A chill ran down her spine and warmth grew in her chest. She shouldn't surrender to her passion, she knew it was wrong and she should wait until they married. She had promised her parents she would not go too far. But he had asked her to be his wife so surely it wouldn't matter. No one had to know except for them. It would be their secret.

Closing her eyes, she let herself go in the moment, she placed her head on his chest, feeling his warmth. She could hear his rapidly beating heart and embedded this moment in her memory forever. They would make their commitment to each other here today. She would be his and he would be hers in love.

CHAPTER 40

DECEMBER 1960

Jimmy had spent so much time with her. They were together every chance they had. She had fallen totally in love with him. He was so attentive to her and made her feel so special. Two months ago he had asked her to marry him and she had said yes. But when they had told her parents about the engagement they had said a firm no. She was still too young to be married. She had a career to think of and a job offer in Canberra next year. They would accept a long engagement and when she was eighteen, if they still wanted to marry then they would give their blessing.

She had not told them that on the day that he had proposed, that they had made love in the shed on the island. It was her very first time ever with a man but she loved him and he loved her. Rose wanted to be with Jimmy for the rest of her life. She had been feeling sick over the last few weeks and her period was now three weeks late. She had no choice. She had to tell her mother that she had disobeyed her wishes.

Now she sat in the doctor's office with her mother. Loretta was not happy. She had warned Rose about what could happen if she was intimate with a man and now her fears had been realised. Rose was pregnant. Her daughter was only fifteen and a half and would be a mother a few months after her sixteenth birthday. She hoped Jimmy would stand by her and love her and take good care of her just like Martin had done for her.

"Well Rose, it looks like you will have to get married now. And very soon, before you start to show. I am not happy about this but, you are my daughter and I will support you in any way I can. Come on, let's go home and tell your father. He is not going to like this at all. Especially as this means you will have to give up your chance of the government job in Canberra." Her mother went silent and lost in her thoughts as they drove back to the farm.

Rose knew her father would be angry and most definitely disappointed in her, but she didn't care. She was going to marry Jimmy. She loved him and she was going to spend the rest of her life with him. She placed a hand on her belly. She could not believe that inside of her was a tiny miracle growing and created by the love they had shared that day. They were having a baby. They would be married and have their own little home and family. Her fairytale was just beginning. Or was it?

THANK YOU

I would like to thank the following people

My big sister Rosemary – Thanks for your suggestions to my novel they added more depth and character. For supporting, loving and always encouraging me and giving me a shove sometimes when I needed it.

To all my family and friends you know who you are – Thank you for supporting me, believing in me and always being there for me.

Mark Connors for my websites and computer help etc I'd be lost without you.

My Amazing MUM – Thank you for choosing me to be your baby girl.

I hope I have become half the woman you are. You are my inspiration and you never judge me, even when I take the wrong turn in life (which can be quite often). No matter what I do you are there beside me, supporting me always. I love you. XXX

AUTHOR BIO

Marianne Delaforce is an adventurous, brave, take-no-prisoners kind of woman with a big heart. Marianne grew up on a dairy farm at Telegraph Point, NSW. She has raised two sons and has four grandchildren.

Marianne will have a go at anything if it interests her and believes if you're not happy and don't like what you're doing, don't whinge about it, change it! She can drive a road train, ride a motorbike, likes skydiving and bungy jumping.

She has worked as a shop assistant, waitress, axeman on the Forest Commission, sales rep, remote camp cook, furniture removalist and truck driver. She has owned and operated a transport company employing forty staff driving twelve trucks out of two depots, one each in NSW and NT. She has also owned and operated a Mediterranean restaurant on the riverbank of Port Macquarie. Over the past thirty-five years her real passion has been singing and entertaining. She currently works as a marriage celebrant, entertainer and audiobook narrator.

She sold her company and restaurant in 2014, packed up and took off on the adventure of a lifetime to find herself again on the "Free, Fabulous and 50 Tour". Marianne has travelled Australia with her trusty blue heeler dog, Elly, by her side. Towing an off-road caravan with her Land Rover, they have made their way around Australia three times, through the Gulf of Carpentaria, up to Cape York, across the Nullarbor, and have traversed both The Gibb River Road and The Outback Way, Australia's longest shortcut.

"The Promised Land" is Marianne's first novel in the series "Promises".

Website: www.mariannedelaforce.com

BROKEN PROMISES
Book 2

At the age of 15, Rose realised her life was going to be very different to the dreams she had once held for her future. She would not live the fairytale life she had imagined. Instead, she would find herself living in a nightmare of broken promises with no apparent way out. But in her deep love for her children she would find the strength, determination and courage to go on, to push forward, if only for them.

Australia is a big, diverse country and Rose experienced many emotions moving around this dynamic landscape more often than she liked. Finding out her mother's secret, and then losing her mother, threw her life into turmoil. To discover more and find answers to the many questions she had, she would have to leave her quiet little village on the mid north coast of New South Wales and travel alone to Italy.

Separated by time and secrets, would strangers finally find each other? And just how long is the road to happiness?

A PROMISE KEPT
BOOK 3

Once upon a time a handsome prince...... that's how fairytales start, and they always end with a happily ever after. With a tough childhood and an abusive father, then several bad choices with men, Lilly's life was far from the fairytale she had always dreamed of.
Lilly felt blessed to have strong women to show her the way, her Grandmother Loretta and her mother Rose. With their love and support she knew she could con-

quer anything, as long as she believed in herself. Even with that support sometimes she wondered, how do you pick yourself up when someone you love is always trying to drag you down and crush your spirit? Why does she continue to allow this to happen?

What was her purpose in life? Lilly sold everything and headed off, driving around Australia to find herself. Traveling alone to some of the most remote parts of Australia she wondered, would she ever find real love? The kind that her grandparents had shared. Did she have the strength and courage to see this bold journey through alone?

Lilly made herself a promise, but would she be able to keep it?